The Temporary Duchess

A Jet City Billionaire Romance

Gina Robinson

THREE JAYS PRESS, LLC

SEATTLE, WASHINGTON

www.ginarobinson.com

Publisher's Note: This is a work of fiction. Names, characters, places, and incidents are a product of the author's imagination. Locales and public names are sometimes used for atmospheric purposes. Any resemblance to actual people, living or dead, or to businesses, companies, events, institutions, or locales is completely coincidental.

Book Layout ©2013 BookDesignTemplates.com
Cover Design by Jeff Robinson

The Temporary Duchess, The Billionaire Duke Series/Gina Robinson. — 1st ed.
ISBN 978-0692673829

THE AGENT EX SERIES
"Full of laughter, intrigue, and, of course, steamy spies." —*RT Book Reviews*

THE SPY WHO LEFT ME
DIAMONDS ARE TRULY FOREVER
LIVE AND LET LOVE
LICENSE TO LOVE
LOVE ANOTHER DAY

CHAPTER ONE

*S*eattle, Washington
Haley Hamilton
Sometimes dreams come true. But would mine? Would I become duchess and save my sister? Find true love with the handsome duke? Live happily ever after? Or would Lady Rose snatch my duke away from me?

The beds in Wareswood Castle were sumptuous and comfortable. Deep and fluffy. Made for sinking in and reveling in complete luxury. Even so, I woke early on Sunday morning after tossing and turning most of the night. Bruised by my dreams as if there had been the proverbial pea beneath my mattress.

My sleep had been haunted by nightmarish images of Riggins proposing to Rose. This might be my last taste of the good life. Worse—it could very well be the end of my hopes for a relationship with Riggins. It sounded melodramatic to say, but my heart would be crushed. For so many reasons.

Riggins. Even his name dancing in my mind made me smile. I had it bad for him. Today was the day. I *had* to win his favor.

I allowed myself the comfort of lounging in bed, snuggling in beneath the covers, daydreaming about him.

A knock on my bedroom door interrupted the rare and lazy pleasure of lying in bed later than dawn. Sid was still asleep in her adjoining room. Which meant I had to answer it.

I got up groggily. My pajama pants were wrinkled and pushed up around my knees. My hair stood on end. My teeth were unbrushed. I ran my fingers through the tangles of my hair, threw on a fluffy robe that came with the room, and paused just before automatically throwing the door open. I had a second of panic, and delight, an awkward combination, that it might be Riggins. Or maybe the highly proper Mr. Thorne.

I was about to ask, *Who's there?* when the knocking started again.

"Haley? Haley, it's Rose. Are you there?"

There was no point in hiding out and ignoring her. She'd find me. She'd already interrupted my thoughts of Riggins. What more damage could she do?

I sighed, heavily, and mentally hissed Rose's name, before gently cracking the door and peeking out at her. She was immaculately turned out—hair flowing in dark waves, makeup done, lightly perfumed, and wearing skintight jeans and a sweater. She even had false eyelashes on. Who wears false eyelashes on the weekend? Or any day at this early hour? Personally, if I ever became duchess, or came into those several hundred million, I was going to get lash extensions and not worry about false lashes again. Rose looked ready for a photo shoot or the latest batch of paparazzi to pop out of the bushes and snap her picture.

She was unreal. I half thought she must be made of wax or something, her skin was so perfect. Maybe she was enchanted and a real woman lurked beneath if the spell was ever broken. In the meantime, my chin itched, which meant I was getting a pimple.

"There you are!" She let out a whoosh of breath. "You're in, thank goodness. May I come in? This is an emergency, I'm afraid." For being in supposed crisis mode, she sounded way too cool and collected.

If this was how she handled dire circumstances, I wanted to be her. There was nothing I could do. This was an emergency, after all. *Exaggerator.* I swung the door open and let her in, closing the door behind us and wondering what kind of emergency she could possibly be having.

She looked around the room, taking everything in. "Isn't your room quaint? You must have a view of the garden. There's not a bad view in the house. I can see the lake from mine."

Yes, and I wished she'd go jump in it, but was too polite to say so aloud. She was clearly hinting that she was Riggins' favorite, since he'd assigned the rooms.

And she had a lake view while I had to make do with the garden. At least he hadn't given her an adjoining one to his.

I forced myself to smile. "There are only two adjoining suites in the castle and this is the best of them." Why was I defending our room assignment to her? "Our rooms were Helen's. At least, that's what Beth told us yesterday.

"How lucky for you. Unfortunately, my room is the American-themed one. All the red, white, and blue, and Americana." She shuddered. "I had to get out of there before I went crackers."

Ha! I almost laughed aloud. Riggins did have a sense of humor.

"Did you have any luck tracking down Helen's mom's ghost last night? Lazer came well equipped for the hunt." I put a small amount of innuendo in my voice, hinting that Lazer had been on the hunt for more than ghosts.

To be honest, I'd been rooting for him to win her affections and take her out of the game. In this weird case, Lazer was my ally. I would have done anything to help him. I watched Rose closely, hoping to see Lazer had disengaged her attention from Riggins.

"Lazer's sweet." She smiled, but I didn't see any glint of lust in it.

Crap. Lazer was losing this battle. Wasn't one billionaire as good as another? Maybe not when one had an obligation to marry within the week and the other seemed to enjoy playing the field. Maybe that was the full attraction of Riggins. That and the title. To someone like Rose, from an aristocratic British family, I supposed being a duchess was important.

"But as a ghost-hunting prodigy?" She shook her head. "I've seen better with the ghost hunters who've come to Papa's house over the years. Lazer and I came up empty." She looked neither surprised nor particularly disappointed.

"I haven't good luck with ghosts. They're surprisingly shy around me. Which is surprising, since so few people are. My father's ancestral home is supposedly haunted, but I've never come close to seeing anything vaguely paranormal. Though Papa claims he has, mostly when he was a boy. I think that's boyish imagination and purely fanciful thinking on his part." She shrugged again.

Hmmmm, I thought. I wasn't surprised. "Ghosts, I suppose, are more commonplace in England. Call me chicken, but I actually have *no* desire to run into one."

"Which exactly means you will! That's how ghosts work, isn't it? You'd better avoid Witham House." Rose's smile was simply too sweet. "It has a reputation for having an active dead community. Ghost stories abound about it! According to historical accounts, several of the early earls met untimely ends. And I wouldn't be surprised if Riggins' Dead Duke has joined the cast. Witham House has an entire tower called the Ghost Tower, and for good reason."

It was clear Rose would use any method at her disposal to scare me off from Riggins.

I ignored her bait. "You said something about an emergency?" Which I was beginning to believe was manufactured just so she could get me out of bed before I had my full beauty rest.

It was one of those odd things, but on days when I didn't have to get up early to go to the bakery, I could sleep until noon. My natural sleep rhythms didn't align with the baker's life and hours.

"Oh! Yes. A female emergency—you don't have a tampon or pad on you, do you? You or Sid? I obviously can't ask Kayla. She'd be no help. I'm afraid things sneaked up on me. I'm all off schedule and still on London time." She laughed. "I hate to ask someone to run out and buy some for me. One or two would get me through to the afternoon."

I thought about playing dumb and telling her we were both completely tampon-free. But I noted her sense of entitlement, as in she wouldn't be dashing off to buy them. She'd send someone else off to do it. And, for good or ill, I had the natural sympathy of a woman caught unprepared.

"I'm sure I have one in my purse." I turned toward the dresser and grabbed my purse to rummage through it. "Ah! Here's one. It's only slightly banged up from bouncing around the bottom of my bag. But it should do."

I turned around to hold it out to her. Rose was standing in front of my open closet, examining my wardrobe, gently fingering one of the dresses I'd decided not to wear last night. And from her posture, she wasn't pleased. She was battle-ready.

She turned to face me. "You brought rather a lot of clothes for this weekend." Her voice was neutral, pleasant, but she couldn't completely mask her surprise. There was that tone that said she hadn't thought I was a clotheshorse and was amazed I knew how to put together a reasonable ensemble.

"And why not?" I laughed lightly. "I shop at Flashionista. Which allows me to afford way more than the average person. I couldn't make up my mind. I just threw a bunch of things in."

Okay, bad me, rubbing it in. I left out the part about having personal Flashionista shoppers provided by Riggins. That was just salt in the wound. I wasn't *that* cruel, though I wanted to be.

Rose frowned as if it had just now occurred to her that if she wanted to win Riggins' favor, maybe she should be shopping at his company. Well, duh. Common sense, right? Even though being a bargain shopper was probably beneath her.

"Let me check with Sid," I said, returning to the original emergency. "I bet she has a tampon or two she can donate to the cause. I'll be right back."

I slid into Sid's room without knocking. She sat up in bed, sleepily, looking sultry and exotically beautiful. Her dark, straight hair was completely smooth, with no sign of bedhead. Some guy was going to be very lucky to wake up to her morning after morning. I couldn't help being a tiny bit jealous. I never woke looking like that. I always looked more like the Bride of Frankenstein.

"What's up?" She stretched her arms high above her head. "Am I late getting up already? I thought breakfast goes until eleven?"

"Rose needs an emergency tampon."

"There's a pouch of them in my bag on the bathroom counter. Take as many as she needs."

I arched an eyebrow.

Sid laughed and whispered, "Take one less than she needs."

"That's better." I winked and went to the bathroom to get them.

I returned to my room, waving a trio of tampons like they were the grand prize package of the weekend.

"Sid had three supers she could spare for the—"

Rose had her hand on the handle of my bedroom door. She struck a pose and threw it open theatrically...

"Rose?" Riggins stood in the open doorway with his hand in his pocket, looking stunned and surprised as his gaze bounced between Rose and the tampon-waving madwoman, me.

Yeah, waving tampons was surely the way to a man's heart. Because men felt so comfortable around feminine protection. Thoughts of menstruation surely turned them on—not. And even though Rose was the one on the rag, I was the one with the pimple on my chin. She couldn't have set me up any better if she'd planned it. And maybe she had.

My face burned. I stuffed the offending super tampons into my robe pocket.

Riggins recovered quickly and smiled in a way that made my heart thump oddly out of rhythm. Like he was mildly amused by the situation. And a little frustrated.

I thought I saw his fist clench in his pocket around something. Something suspiciously square in outline. If we'd been alone, I would have asked him if that was a jewelry box in his pocket or was he just happy to see me. All right, that was a little presumptuous, maybe. Or optimistic. Hope does spring eternal.

I did wonder, though. This weekend was clearly a test. *Was* he going to crown one of us with Helen's ring by the end? If so, the end was quickly approaching. Or was he just toying with us?

"Riggins! What are you doing here?" A seductive smile lit Rose's face.

If she was displeased about him stopping by *my* room, she didn't show it. And the traitor completely ignored the tampons and the trouble I'd gone to to get them for her, her emergency completely forgotten.

"I could ask you the same thing." He smiled pleasantly at her and looked around her to me.

I should have done a better job finger-combing my hair. I looked a mess. In a head-to-head competition with Lady Rose, I was so far behind, I came in third even though there were only two of us in the running. I resisted the urge to duck behind the bed.

"I stopped by to see if Haley wanted to go down to breakfast with me," Riggins said.

"Great minds think alike." Rose took his arm. "I stopped by for the same reason."

Big, fat liar!

"As you can see, Haley isn't quite ready. I'll walk down with you." She gently turned him around, calling back over her shoulder to me as she took his arm, "Join us when you can, Haley!"

Riggins

Rose saved me from making a tactical mistake. On second thought, surprising Haley in her room with a proposal wasn't the most romantic gesture. Or even real clear thinking on my part. Wasn't I the guy who'd refused to propose in a lawyer's office? I had to do better than dragging a woman out of bed to propose a business marriage to her.

Even though this was anything *but* the romance of the century, Haley deserved to be proposed to when she was at least wide awake and looking her best. Not waving a set of tampons around. Which made me chuckle. She looked so cute when she blushed. I wanted her to be clearheaded enough to weigh the pros and cons of what I was proposing.

I thought Haley looked adorable in her rumpled pajamas and bedhead hair, blushing beautifully as she flashed those tampons. Which were obviously for Rose, who hadn't blushed at all. But there was no way to convince a woman she looked hot when she was convinced she didn't.

Rose clung to me through breakfast like an anxious child. Probably worried that if she lost sight of me for a second, I'd offer my hand to Haley. She hung on my every word. Looked at me adoringly. And flirted with me very prettily.

Some guys would have eaten her attention up. I couldn't imagine spending any part of my life being constantly fawned over like that. It must have been the practical upbringing by my no-nonsense mom. And the last thing *I* wanted was to be chased around by photographers who'd been tipped off by Rose about where we were going to be every minute of our lives.

I'd managed to keep the media away from us over the weekend by hiring the best security crew in Seattle to patrol the perimeter of the grounds and keep the riffraff away. They were the same company Flash used. But I'd asked for a double security team and added the extra drone-combating detail to the package. Life married to Rose for any length of time would be one interruption into my private life after another.

Maybe I did share some DNA with the reclusive Dead Duke, after all. His private life out of the spotlight sounded damn appealing after the week I'd had.

Before Haley came down to breakfast, Thorne pulled me aside, asking for a private meeting, saving me from Rose's constant attention.

I excused myself and left her in Lazer's capable hands while I met with Thorne behind closed doors in the library.

"This is a very good room, Your Grace." Thorne looked around at the leather-bound volumes on the shelves. "Not as nice, or as large, as Witham House's. But a very nice collection, all the same. I frequently met with the late duke in the library. It and his study were his favorite rooms. I must say, I quite like the idea of continuing the tradition with the current generation."

I fell in to a deep leather armchair. "Enough beating around the bush, Thorne. What did you want to talk to me about?"

"I wanted to discuss the details of the DNA results."

"Yes, I've read them," I said, trying to keep the annoyance out of my voice.

"Did you understand them?"

I nodded. "Enough to know Rose's claims are accurate—she is descended from the late duchess."

Thorne held my gaze. "Very distantly, sir. So remotely it's like that game—the six degrees of Kevin Bacon. You comprehend the difficulty it presents. There will be hundreds of young women who could make the same claim. You won't be safe until you're married."

"I'm not the one who wrote the will." I fought to remain calm. "Your Dead Duke wasn't as smart as he thought."

"He was smart enough," Thorne said. "His last wishes were clearly that you should marry the duchess' *nearest* descendant. That's Haley. The DNA results prove it conclusively."

I leveled my gaze at Thorne, looking him directly in the eyes. "And just how the hell is she so closely related?"

"I think you know the answer to that, sir."

My phone rang, interrupting our conversation. I pulled it out and glanced at the caller ID. My CFO.

"I believe you should take that, Your Grace."

I set my jaw.

"Shall I give you some privacy?"

"Stay. I have the feeling you know what this is about, anyway." I picked up the call. Ten minutes later, I'd talked our CFO down off the ledge. Rumors were already flying in the financial markets of a possible dump of Flash shares on the market by an unhappy investor. We all knew who that was.

This was clearly the Dead Duke's work.

"Rattling your saber?" I said to Thorne when I hung up from my call.

"You have less than a week to get married, sir. I wouldn't delay. Propose to Miss Hamilton and get it over with." He paused. "We'll need her to meet with our doctor, of course, the morning of the wedding. To make sure she fulfills all the terms and isn't pregnant. And she'll have to sign a waiver releasing her medical report to us.

"Washington State requires a three-day waiting period after applying for the license. You have no time to lose."

"Lady Rose is going to be a problem," I said.

"Let me handle her, sir. That's what I'm here for."

CHAPTER TWO

H *aley*
By the time Sid and I came down to breakfast, the dining room was empty. Justin and Kayla were out for a walk around the grounds. Lazer was working on his laptop in the morning room. Riggins was meeting with Thorne in the library. Rose had apparently returned to her room for one reason or another. Probably to avoid conflict with me, the little traitor. Little did she know I was pretty conflict averse.

Sid was tired and unusually pale this morning. She was out of breath from simply descending the stairs, and complained of a headache. I watched her closely for signs she was slipping back into a horrible bout of anemia. They sometimes came on so gradually we barely noticed them until she was in a full-on assault. And sometimes they attacked out of the blue, pouncing on her overnight.

I didn't see any signs of a rash or a bunch of unexplained bruises. Which was only minimally reassuring. She didn't have *all* the symptoms, just many of them. She waved off my concerns. But everything else made me leery. A nineteen-year-old shouldn't tire from walking down the stairs. Even a simple headache was a symptom and put me on edge.

Time was wasting for all of us. I needed that cure. I needed it *now*. At the very least, I needed to know if it existed for sure. I needed those Chinese connections Mr. Thorne had flaunted. I needed the money and the power the Dead Duke could provide.

I ate my breakfast and helped Sid back to bed. She claimed her tiredness was nothing more than being awakened too early. Nineteen-year-olds still needed lots of sleep. I thought she protested too much.

The morning was clear and beautiful, especially for February, with none of the fog that had recently plagued us. The temperature was already nearly fifty. Very warm for this time of year. I grabbed a few pieces of bread from the breakfast buffet and headed out for a walk along the lake. I thought I'd feed the ducks and clear my head.

I hadn't gotten far down the path to the lake when I heard footsteps behind me.

Mr. Thorne called out to me, "Miss Hamilton!"

I stopped short and turned around, catching him waving at me. I waved back. When he reached me, he was slightly out of breath. I hoped he wasn't coming down with anemia, too. Though, in his case, I assumed it was more to do with middle-aged-out-of-shapeness. "Haley." I smiled at him. "You have to call me Haley. Everyone else does."

"Soon I hope I'll be calling you duchess."

It was sweet and disconcerting to hear the genuine warmth and sincerity in his voice. It caught me off guard. I thought of Mr. Thorne as the enemy, at times. And at other times, an unlikely ally. But not as a friend. I smiled back at him. "That's completely up to Riggins, I think."

"Is it?"

I didn't answer. What could I say?

"Mind if I walk with you a bit? I wouldn't mind seeing some of the grounds. And I'd like a word, if I may."

"Not at all," I said. "I was just going to the lake." I inhaled the cool air deeply, feeling sentimental and curious. "I've been trying to picture growing up here. What would life have been like for Helen? Did she ever imagine she'd grow up to be a duchess?" I laughed, nervously, as I realized what I was saying. "Well, who *would* imagine they'd grow up to be a duchess? Not me."

"You're much too modest, and it wasn't part of your world," Mr. Thorne said. "But I imagine Helen had high aspirations from the beginning. A woman's place, in those days, was dependent upon the status of their husband. Helen's family had new wealth and power here in the States. But they would have longed for the respectability of the old families. The prestige of a title, like so many families in their day did.

"I'm quite certain, from the stories I've heard, that she was raised knowing she would marry an important man. Quite possibly a titled Englishman. Though dukes were a rare enough quantity, even in those days. I would imagine, though, she quite dreamed of being a countess and leaving home to manage a large estate household.

"England's climate isn't so very different from here. We have our share of rain, too. She probably imagined she'd be right at home. At least, that's what her parents would have assured her."

I nodded as we walked, me with my napkin full of bread. What he said made perfect sense. "How does Wareswood compare to Witham House? You've been there often. I'd like your opinion. Would Helen have been impressed by the size of her new estate? Should I be afraid of the task of helping run it, if Riggins chooses me."

"Oh, yes, Helen would have been mightily impressed, I'm sure. Witham House quite easily outshines Wareswood in almost every aspect. Remember, Wareswood was built with the brick from one of the duke's lesser estates.

"Wareswood is merely quaint in comparison to the grandeur of Witham House. House is a misnomer, really. It's more a castle. You haven't been curious and looked it up online?"

"Oh, I've been curious. The pictures scare me. I can't imagine really living in a castle. But pictures can be deceiving. I wanted to hear what you thought."

His head bobbed. "I feel quite certain Helen's parents were thrilled at the match she made. Even though it put their daughter out of their league and social class, it was a parenting job well done."

I nodded. "Funny, isn't it—little girls dream of being princesses. No one really imagines being a real-life duchess. And yet it scares the crap out of me. I don't think I'm cut out for it."

"The late duke thought you were."

It was nice of Mr. Thorne to say so, even if he did have an ulterior motive. We reached the lake and stopped to admire it.

"I'm not sure whether I should be creeped out or complimented by the late duke's surreptitious attention. I can't imagine what he saw in me to impress him. Other than my bloodline, and that's a tenuous connection. I'm not that closely related to him."

"Family loyalty, I should imagine," Mr. Thorne said. "And strength in overcoming adversity, losing your parents so young and stepping up to care for your sister. Don't sell yourself short, Haley. Those are qualities not everyone possesses. You put yourself through college and now you're helping your sister when you could be off playing and enjoying yourself."

"But isn't that what anyone would do?" I stared out over the calm water. Not even a ripple broke the glassy surface.

"No, it's not. I hate to say it, but it's not. It's rarer than you might imagine."

"That's nice of you to say." I smiled at him, watching the ducks across the lake, wondering when they'd see me and come begging for the bread I'd brought. "You said you wanted a word?"

"Yes." He hesitated. "I heard your sister was tired this morning. Is she feeling unwell?"

"She gets like this from time to time. Every time I worry she's relapsing. With every minute and every relapse, her chances for a long, healthy life diminish. Fatigue is a symptom of the anemia. Sometimes it flares up, even when she's technically in remission. If we're lucky, it's just a blip and doesn't bloom into the a full-length episode of the disease."

He looked genuinely sympathetic. "I have some experience with degenerative family illnesses. I'm sorry." He paused, looking like he was debating with himself.

"Yes?" I prompted him.

"I shouldn't tell you this. I don't want to get your hopes up. But I like both you and your sister. More so the more I get to know you. Seeing you together this weekend has made me feel guilty for being the late duke's instrument."

His voice cracked very slightly. "I hope you realize that I'm not a bad fellow, really. I'm as forced into my role as you are into yours."

I stared at him. I'd never thought he'd been forced into doing the Dead Duke's bidding. I'd assumed it was just a job. It was on the tip of my tongue to ask him what the Dead Duke had on him, but I thought better of it. He was a very private man. "No, I never thought you were—"

"How could you not?" His smile was soft. "You're too kind. I'd like to help you and Sid out, Haley. Which is why I feel compelled to tell you what I believe I know. And I say I believe I know only because there's a chance I could be wrong. That I misheard. And that's one of the reasons I haven't brought it up before. If I'm wrong...well, I hope I'm not." He held my gaze.

I held my breath.

"There's a sibling," he said at last. "Your sister has a full sibling. A twin."

My knees went weak. Mr. Thorne caught my arm to steady me.

"No! Are you sure?"

"As I said, not completely. I overhead the duke talking to one of his investigators about it several months before his death. I wasn't supposed to know. The records are sealed. But I believe there are clues at Witham House among the late duke's papers to your sister's twin's identity."

"Does my sister's twin know about my sister? Is this twin an identical twin?" My mind raced along with my pulse. An identical twin would have to be a perfect match. But if they were identical, would they also have the disease? Would it be another dead end? In any case, even a fraternal twin would be a full sibling.

"I don't know...Haley." He studied the lake a minute, concentrating as if trying to remember details. "I have to admit to being an eavesdropper." He glanced at me with an embarrassed look on his face. "And not a very good one. But my impression is no. Whoever the twin is, they don't know about Sid."

"Can you help me find them? Do you know any more?" I would plead with him if I had to.

He shook his head. "Only what I've told you. And I've told you more than I should. I wanted you to know the full amount of what may be at stake. It's quite possibly more than just the late duke's help to find a cure. It may very well *be* the cure.

"I only have the authority to release certain funds and information to you in accordance with the terms of the late duke's will. And although I'm the late duke's agent, I can't act completely alone. There's a committee that has oversight on me.

"The duke was very thorough. And, as I said, secretive. He believed in redundancy and leaving as little as humanly possible to chance. There are sealed papers that I have instructions to give you as soon as certain terms are met."

I could guess what those were.

"It would be my guess, and hope, that one of those contains the twin's identity."

I couldn't get over this new information. It was what we'd been hoping for. And yet...Sid had a twin. A real biological twin. I couldn't help feeling jealous. How would this change things between us? It had never mattered to me that she was adopted. But would it matter to her that she now had a blood sibling? Was blood truly thicker than water?

Mr. Thorne still had a grip on my arm. He squeezed gently. "Marry the new duke. Give him an heir as soon as may be. And I'm fairly certain the prize will be the identity of Sid's twin.

"In the meantime, you need to get to Witham House. You may find something there among all the late duke's files and paperwork. Being a mother to a future duke isn't the worst thing in the world."

I bit my lip, still reeling from the revelation. What did I do now?

"Don't let Lady Rose snatch the new duke from you. I will, of course, aid you in any way possible. But you must marry the duke. And it must be a *real* marriage. With everything that goes along with it, including, and maybe most importantly, children. Whether he wants them or not is immaterial. It's the quickest way to Sid's cure."

Mr. Thorne paused again. "I hope it wasn't wrong of me to tell you my suspicions. And I hope I'm not mistaken in all this. But my conscience wouldn't let me keep silent any longer.

"This remains between us, though, you understand? You can't tell your sister. Or anyone. Especially the duke. I am, officially, in his employ now, and his agent as well as the late duke's. It's a strange relationship to be working on both sides, especially with the new duke considering me the adversary.

"Working with you and revealing what I have to you could get me fired and destroy the impeccable professional career and reputation I've spent my adult life building. You understand?"

I nodded. "Of course. You have my word." But how would I keep such news secret?

"Good, then." The lines of his face softened with relief. "I'll leave you to your thoughts. I have to get back to the house and waylay Lady Rose before she causes more trouble." He grinned.

I watched him walk back down the path, heart hammering in my chest, hope truly springing and mind whirling along with my emotions. I'd never even dared to hope Sid had a *twin*. That seemed too fantastical. But if she did, our lives were going to be upended. I couldn't also help being a little envious. What would it be like to find out I had another sibling somewhere? Someone I'd shared a womb with? Why had Sid never felt the presence of a twin? Wasn't that supposed to be common? And how could a mother split her twins up? Leaving at least one of them at an orphanage, abandoned on the steps?

The quacking of ducks startled me out of my thoughts. Now that Mr. Thorne had gone, the ducks had noticed me. Was Mr. Thorne that unapproachable and so scary he'd kept even ducks at bay? And was he telling the truth? Could I believe him? Or was this another diabolical ploy instigated by the Dead Duke to get me to comply with his wishes? Was Mr. Thorne playing good cop to the Dead Duke's bad?

I considered myself a decent judge of character. But I had no experience with this level of deceit, manipulation, and trickery. I wondered—could I really keep the knowledge of a possible twin from Sid? Was that fair? On the other hand, was it right to get her hopes up if Mr. Thorne was mistaken? What if I couldn't produce a boy, an heir? Would the Dead Duke be so cruel as to withhold this potentially lifesaving information from Sid and me forever? And was it right to marry a man, assuming I could, and get pregnant just to save my sister? Was Mr. Thorne right—there were worse things than being a duchess and mother to a future duke? There was so much to think about. So much to test my morals and values and beliefs in the kind of person I was.

As a gentle breeze kicked up, I pulled a piece of bread from the napkin, squatted at the edge of the water, and held it out to entice the ducks, tearing off little pieces and throwing them into the water as the ducks approached. I grinned as I watched them snap the soggy bread bits out of the water and quack happily. If only my life were so simple.

The sound of a snapping twig startled me. At first, I thought Mr. Thorne was returning. I looked up into the dark, sexy eyes of Riggins, Duke of Witham, and my heart nearly stopped. Yes, there were much worse things in life than being married to this particularly hot billionaire duke. Unfortunately, all rational thought had fled my mind. I couldn't think of anything—either better or worse. I was lost in Riggins' intense gaze.

Riggins

I sneaked up on Haley and startled her. That hadn't been my intent. I'd been watching her from a distance as she fed the ducks and I worked up my nerve to seal my fate. There was something serene and beautiful about her movements and the way she blended with the calm, natural surroundings. It reminded me, for the hundredth time, of my younger, less complicated self and young, relatively uncomplicated love.

I had the ring in my pocket. Thorne was keeping Rose out of the way. I'd met him on the path to the lake.

He'd pointed me to Haley. "Make your move now, sir. She's ripe for it. And remember, this has to be a real marriage with *all* that involves." He lifted his eyebrows to emphasize his point.

I'd nearly laughed. Did he think that would be a hardship for me, at least?

It was Haley I worried about. Her heart. Mine was jaded enough that I wasn't convinced the tiny stirring noises it was making could ever flame into a great love again. Despite the temptations she presented, I was still only planning to make her my temporary duchess while I bought more time to get out of this mess. There had to be a way.

I wasn't arrogant, but it wasn't impossible that she'd fall in love with her husband, me. And what then? Did I want to be responsible for killing the romantic illusions of someone else? And yet...

And yet nothing, I told myself. Maybe I was being an egotistical prick. I hated to interrupt her solitude, but the ring was burning a hole in my pocket, the morning was waning, and our guests would soon be leaving. I stepped on a twig as I approached.

She looked up. My heart caught. The look in her eyes. Damn, it was enough to turn me to mush.

"Sorry. Am I disturbing you? Thorne said I'd find you here."

"You're not disturbing *me*. I'm not so sure about the ducks. But I'm out of bread, anyway. And pretty sure these guys will turn traitor on me quickly enough once they discover I'm empty-handed." She shook the crumbs from a paper napkin into the water.

The ducks dove after them and quacked and fluttered, begging for more.

"Sorry, guys!" She held out her empty hands and laughed as they paddled away. "So much for loyalty! Was I right?"

She stood and faced me. "The weekend has been fantastic. Thank you. I'm only sorry that it's flown by so quickly and tomorrow I'll have to return to work and regular life."

I took a step toward her and caught her soft, small hand in mine. "Will you? I'm not so sure about that. The weekend isn't over yet. I still have one offer to make."

I pulled the ring box from my pocket, opened it, and balanced it on my open palm like an offering to a water nymph. She looked so damn beautiful with the breeze blowing her silvery hair over her face, rippling the previously calm water behind her. She could have been the lady of the lake risen from the deep.

She stared at the open box, not quite sure if I was serious or what I was suggesting.

"Will you marry me, Haley? And be my temporary duchess for as long as it takes to foil the Dead Duke's dastardly plans for us?"

Her gaze bounced between the ring and me. "That's an unconventional marriage proposal. Not exactly how I imagined a guy doing the job."

"Should I get down on one knee?" She laughed softly and shook her head. "Do dukes get down on one knee when proposing to commoners? That must go against protocol."

"May I remind you—on American soil I'm only Riggins, commoner, completely at your mercy and your disposal." I smiled an idiot sort of grin. She did that to me. Made me feel light and happy, almost against my will, like a drug that ran through my veins. "We both know this will be an unconventional marriage."

"Will it?" She grinned lopsidedly. "Before I answer, I have to ask—will it be a *real* marriage? With everything that marriage generally entails? Mr. Thorne seems to think consummating it is part of the deal."

I couldn't tell her thoughts on the matter. The idea excited me. In fact, thoughts of making love to her had invaded even my dreams this weekend. And before. There was something about her...

And why shouldn't we have fun? We were young and healthy.

"Thorne's been talking to you about sex?" I shook my head, amused at the thought of the staid, reserved solicitor bringing up the birds and the bees. "I thought it was only me he had the talk with." I couldn't help running with the gag. "He made some vague allusions to respecting you and taking time to let things progress naturally."

"He did not!" She looked adorable as she laughed again. "You haven't answered my question."

"Yes, it will have to be real. Especially, given the circumstances—"

"You mean my virginity?" Her eyes were clear and dancing with amusement, not embarrassment like I'd expected.

"I will draw the line at anyone inspecting the sheets for blood the morning after the wedding night, but yes, that. The marriage will have to be legal. And to be legal, we'll have to have sex. Lots of it."

I took another step closer to her, catching a whiff of her clean, sexy scent. It was a combination of perfume, soap, and beauty products that was all her own. "You're beautiful, Haley. And it's no secret I'm attracted to you.

"I can't lie and say I'm in love with you. I'm not sure I'll ever fall in love again. But I like you. I feel comfortable with you. We get along. We can be friends with benefits, at least. Most couples can't ask for more."

She pursed her lips. "And the requirement to have an heir?"

I was thinking of the pleasures of having sex with her. Her question caught me up short. "I'm not ready for children. I can't see foisting a dukedom on some poor, unsuspecting baby. Can you?"

She took her time answering. "I don't know. *Maybe.* It would be simpler for both of us if we decided to get right down and attend to duty. Produce the heir and go our ways."

I was still holding the ring in the palm of my hand. I hadn't expected a marriage proposal to involve this much negotiation. "You're probably right. But as I told you before, my dad abandoned me when I was a baby. I swore I'd never do that to a child." My mouth went dry. "I won't consider having a kid unless I can't foil the Dead Duke's plans. Or someone completely steals my heart." Meaning her.

Why the hell had I said that? My heart was as hard as they came. But she'd softened it already.

Her eyes shone with sympathy. "I understand. It's no fun growing up with only one parent. Believe me, I know. Even if that one parent was a good one."

"Then we're agreed. We won't let the Dead Duke force our hand. We won't bring children into anything less than a stable, loving relationship. As for my hand, I'm offering it to you. You haven't answered my question yet—will you marry me?" Why was my heart hammering so loudly?

"Yes." She nodded and smiled sweetly. "I will."

I grinned like an idiot, ear to ear. Why was I so damn happy? Was it only relief? Or was I fooling myself? I pulled the ring from the box and slid it onto the ring finger of her left hand. It was a perfect fit.

She held her hand out to admire it, wiggling her fingers so the diamonds sparkled in the sunlight, and smiled with happiness.

She threw her arms around my neck and looked into my eyes. Her lips were moist and gently parted. "We'll be the happiest temporary couple on the planet."

"Will we?"

"I promise to be the best temporary duchess I can be. And do everything I can to make you temporarily happy. Together we'll conquer the world, in passing, at least, and save my sister. But my sister's salvation has to be permanent."

I brushed the hair out of her face. "You do realize we have to be married within the week. This is going to be a scandalously short engagement. People will talk, and my British fans will be furious."

"Let them eat cake!" She laughed. "*Wedding* cake."

"I can't believe it. The power and title has already gone to your head and we aren't even married yet."

I wrapped my arms around her waist and pulled her close. "We'll have to get the license tomorrow. There's a three-day waiting period before it's valid. Married on Saturday?"

"Five days? Or is it six?" Her eyes went wide. "You want me to plan a wedding in less than a week?"

"Why not? We'll get married at my place. Just close friends. My housekeeper can arrange everything—the flowers and catering, if you give her the menu and let her know your preferences. Or we'll pay a wedding planner. One of the top ones in the city will take us on if we throw enough money at them."

"I can do it if you can. You have to arrange the honeymoon, after all."

"That's easy," I said. "We'll go to Witham House."

"I'm sensing a theme here—staying at one of your many homes. Is that really the dream honeymoon for a duke and duchess?" Her voice was teasing.

"What's more romantic than honeymooning in a private castle? Lots of people would pay good money for that."

She paused. "You have a point. All right, then. I'll have to give my notice at the bakery tomorrow. I work until two. I can go for the license after that. If you want my famous mint brownies, baked especially for you, you'll have to come in early to get them. The Blackberry staff won't be happy I'm not giving two weeks. More like two hours. I'll need every minute I can to plan—"

I lowered my lips to hers, silencing any more wedding talk. A guy should at least get a kiss for the trouble of proposing and handing a woman an expensive antique ring.

The first taste of her made my pulse race. As my tongue slid into her mouth, I wondered what the hell I was doing playing this dangerous game of chicken with my heart. And what was it thinking, beating out of control, as if Haley might be the best thing that had happened to me in a long time?

aley
Looking at my ring, being in Riggins' arms, the thought of being his wife—all made me ridiculously happy. For more reasons than I was willing to analyze at the moment. For both Sid and me. And yet guilt flitted around the edges of my mind. Riggins didn't know what Mr. Thorne had told me about Sid's possible twin. Which gave me a ridiculously strong motive for marrying Riggins, everything else aside. And meant we started our marriage with a secret between us.

Though I'd teased him about honeymooning at Witham House, I was only playing it cool. I couldn't wait to get there and start looking for clues to Sid's sibling. And then there was the plain fact that my crush on Riggins had grown into love.

I had fallen in love with him against my own common sense. But the heart wants what it wants. And mine was no different. I would have wanted Riggins even if he hadn't been filthy rich and titled. In fact, if that were the case, things would have been so much less complicated. We might have even have had a real chance if he was just a regular guy.

When Riggins and I finally broke our kiss, we couldn't stop smiling into each other's eyes. I know I couldn't keep my grin down.

"We should go back to the castle and tell the others." Riggins squeezed me.

I was dying to tell Sid. And Kayla. But Rose...

As if my thoughts had conjured her out of lake mist, we heard footsteps coming down the path. Riggins turned toward them.

Rose appeared around a bend in the path. She squinted into the sun. I could have sworn she scowled when she saw us together. She recovered quickly and shaded her eyes with her hand before waving.

"Is this a private party? Or can anyone join in?" She sounded a little frantic and breathless. Like she'd been trying to stop the inevitable.

But she'd arrived just a fraction of a second too late. The ring was on *my* finger now. And the only way it was coming off was if someone pried it off.

Riggins arched an eyebrow. I stifled a laugh and matched his look, heart racing.

"What's going on here?" Rose approached us.

Riggins grabbed my left hand and flashed the ring on my finger. "This beautiful woman has just agreed to be my wife."

Another scowl quickly crossed Rose's face. She replaced it fast enough with a forced smile that had absolutely no warmth to it.

"You're the first to know." Riggins grinned at me and brushed my lips with a kiss, laying it on thick.

"Lucky me!" She didn't sound lucky at all.

"You have to promise to keep it quiet," Riggins said in a stern voice I'd never heard him use before. "We'll make an official announcement to the press after we've told our friends and family."

The look on Rose's face said it all—she would have to come up with a new scheme to get what she wanted. I wasn't naïve enough to expect her to be a gracious loser and simply fade into the background. But I wondered what her next move would be. Would she still try to contest the will?

"We should get back to the castle, then." Her smile was frozen in place. "So you can share your good news." She was speaking to both of us, but her gaze was on Riggins.

Back at the castle, Riggins called everyone together and ordered champagne all around. He held my hand as a waiter poured. "Haley and I have an announcement. She's agreed to be my duchess." He lifted his champagne glass. "To my beautiful future wife!"

Everyone lifted their glasses in toast.

"And," Riggins said, "consider this your save-the-date announcement. Keep next Saturday afternoon open. You're all invited to the wedding. My place."

"Here or in England, Your Grace," Justin said with a twinkle in his eye. "If it's England, we're out. Kayla's grounded for the duration until the baby comes."

Riggins shook his head. "Here. On Lake Washington just around the lake from you, neighbor."

"In that case, I think we can make it." He winked at his wife.

Mr. Thorne looked happiest of all. Next to Sid, of course.

Kayla was giving me a funny look. She came up to me as the guys crowded around Riggins to give him a bad time about losing his bachelorhood. "Another unconventional marriage. Remind me sometime and I'll give you my pointers for surviving, and thriving, after being thrown into a very unconventional quickie marriage." She laughed.

I wondered what she meant by unconventional. It was no secret her marriage had been spur of the moment. She and Justin had each been in business in Reno for different companies, reconnected after knowing each other in college, and ended up married by the end of the weekend. It was rash, but they were obviously happy together. Was that what she meant by unconventional? If so, it was nothing like Riggins and mine would be—an old-fashioned marriage of convenience. An arranged marriage. A marriage arranged by a dead guy, even. I dared her to top that. But, of course, I kept those thoughts to myself.

Instead, I smiled at her. "I'll hold you to it. I have no
idea how to be a billionaire's wife, let alone a duchess!
I'm a middle-class girl and probably always will be,
deep down."

Her smile matched mine. "I can help you with making the transition from middle class to being married to
a billionaire. It's not so bad really, after you get used to
being with a man who's constantly in the spotlight.
The part about being titled—I've got nothing there."
She hugged me sideways to avoid her pregnant belly.
"I'm sure you'll be wonderful. Because you're kind and
caring and motivated. That's all key.

"One piece of advice—develop a thick skin quickly.
There will be detractors who will say horrible things
everywhere you look, particularly online and in social
media. Trolls who can't stand for anyone to get something more than they have or that they think isn't deserved or earned.

"Ignore them. They're simply jealous. In your case, I
think it may be worse because so many women had
their hopes up and their sights set on him." She slid a
quick glance at Rose.

I nodded and stifled a laugh at her pointed look, not
fully believing I could ever get used to Riggins' lifestyle. "I'll keep that in mind." I hesitated, but my
thoughts tumbled out anyway. "What I really need to
know is how to *stay* married to a man like Riggins."

I couldn't believe I'd just blurted that out. But I figured Kayla knew Riggins as well as anyone. Or at least
her husband did. And I was suddenly desperate for
help. Because even now the thought of my marriage

being temporary broke my heart. It only made sense that the longer we were married, the more devastating losing Riggins would be. But if it lasted for a lifetime...

Kayla studied me closely, clearly trying to read my face.

I didn't try to mask my feelings for Riggins from her. I was in love with him. I hated to admit it, even to myself, but I was. Which seemed ridiculous after so short a time. Didn't love take time to grow? Wasn't that conventional wisdom?

But wasn't it also true that most people knew pretty quickly when they met someone whether they were the kind of person they could marry or not? It was easy enough to discard perfectly nice men because there was no chemistry. And for me, it had as much to do with the meshing of our personalities as with physical lust. So maybe I wasn't too far off base or as crazy as I seemed.

"Oh, I see," she said finally, as if understanding.

Justin knew the real circumstances behind our situation. I didn't know how much he'd told Kayla, if anything. I was taking a chance she knew at least something. And now it was clear she did.

She lifted one eyebrow. "Riggins isn't any more complicated than any other guy. He values loyalty, honesty, and trust. Make yourself indispensable to him. Be the best thing that ever happened to him. Stick by him no matter what.

"Get public opinion on your side early on. Let people live the fairytale vicariously through you and you'll have them hooked. He won't want to be the bad guy.

That's not Riggins' style. Most importantly, treat him so well that he loses his heart and can't imagine life without you." She glanced at Riggins and the guys. "That shouldn't be too hard. There's clearly chemistry between you two."

The baby kicked. She winced. And laughed. "Or get pregnant," she joked. "That pretty much links you forever. In your case, with a boy if at all possible."

I hadn't noticed Rose hovering nearby until then. How much had she overheard? Did it matter? What could she do now?

Anything, I told myself. She was unpredictable, and that worried me more than anything.

After lunch, the party broke up and people headed home. Justin and Kayla left first, followed by Mr. Thorne. Rose played it cool, suddenly attaching herself to Lazer and begging a ride home in the Bentley from him. I didn't trust her, but maybe I was wrong about her. Maybe she had her eye on Lazer now. I wished her luck with that. Lazer was enjoying his freedom too much to give it up for the commitment of marriage. Without his own Dead Duke to force him into matrimony, I didn't see him walking down the aisle anytime soon.

Riggins sent Sid and me home in a car. Sid was still looking peaked, but she was now excited, too.

She seemed happy as she studied me. "You're glowing."

"Why shouldn't I be?" I grinned at her. "I just won the duchess contest. And best yet—we're going to get you your cure!"

I had to bite my tongue to keep from spilling my news to her. Mr. Thorne was probably right that it was best not to get her hopes up. But *I* could revel in the joy of thinking about it and imagining the happy outcome.

"You look really happy." Sid squeezed my hand. "Be careful, sis. You know I love you. I don't want to see you get hurt." She looked suddenly worried.

"Don't worry about me. I can handle myself."

"Can you?" She frowned. "Can you really control your heart? It looks pretty out of control already to me." She leaned her head on my shoulder. "Do you think he loves you?"

"No," I said. "But he likes me very much."

She sighed. "That's something. It's a start. If this were a really good fairytale destined to have the proper ending, we'd seek out an old crone, a witch, and buy a love potion."

"You mean like *The Little Mermaid*?" I said. Sid had always loved that story. "We'd have to lose our tongue for that, I think. Love potions always have a steep price."

"Yes, but is any price too high for true love?"

I leaned my head against hers. "Can true love come from a potion or pill?"

"I want you to be happy, Hale. I don't want him to break your heart. You're more sensitive than you give yourself credit for. The last thing I need is to finally get physically healthy, only to have you slide into depression.

"I know you're trying to hide it from me. In fact, I think you're trying to hide it from yourself. But I've never seen you like this about any guy before. This is different. If Mom were here, I think she'd take one look at you and him and say he's the one, like she did with Aunt Kelly. Or, at least, you think he is."

Aunt Kelly wasn't really our aunt, just a close friend of Mom's. I was surprised Sid remembered that. Mom had taken one look at Aunt Kelly with her new boyfriend of just a few days and blurted to Dad that Kelly was going to marry him. And sure enough, she was right. Mom had that sense about her. The love whisperer. What kind of superpower was that?

For myself, I was glad Mom wasn't here to witness this. I was afraid of what she'd say and the warning she'd give me.

"I'll be fine," I said with more confidence than I felt. "Don't worry. As soon as you're cured, I'll be perfect."

She didn't know how close a cure might be.

The week passed in a whirl and a blur. Liz and Jasmine were nearly deliriously happy for me, especially when I asked them to be bridesmaids in my Saturday wedding. I mean, really, how many chances do you get to be a bridesmaid to a duchess? And involved in such a high-profile wedding? The only downside was having to keep it quiet for now.

I gave my notice to Sally at The Blackberry at the close of my shift on Monday, apologizing profusely, but

saying this had to be my last day. After swearing her to
secrecy, I told her about my engagement.

"To Riggins, the new duke?" She was stunned.

Which didn't say much about her confidence in me.
The bakery had been full of rumors and the competition had been all over the news. I comforted myself by
convincing myself she hadn't expected victory so *soon.*
Or the wedding to be within the week.

I also imagined she was relieved I was leaving. All
the attention on Riggins and me overwhelmed the bakery and upset the regular clientele and relaxed atmosphere The Blackberry prided itself on. Yes, business
boomed. But it was almost overpowering.

"We wish you all the best," she said, gracious to the
end, even though I was leaving her in a lurch. "You
have to let us make your wedding cake. I'll insist on
that! We're the best bakery in the city." She smiled
with pride.

"I'd love that," I said, hesitating. "But the wedding's
Saturday. I'll understand if you can't work me in. I
know how far you're booked ahead."

"Nonsense! For one of our own, we'll make an ex-
ception." She leaned toward me. "And baking a duke's
wedding cake—when will I ever get another chance at
that? Baking a cake for aristocracy is on my bucket list.
You can't deprive me of that.

"How many guests are you expecting? And do you
think Riggins will want at least one chocolate layer
with mint filling? He seems very fond of our chocolate
mint brownies. Maybe we should make a brownie
groom's cake?"

And so one thing, at least, was settled. Once I had a rough count of the number of guests.

After I left the bakery, I hurried home, showered, and changed into one of my new Flashionista dresses. I wanted to look nice when we got our license. I didn't want to give Riggins any reason for second-guessing his choice.

And there was a good chance we'd be recognized. My days of going out without makeup had already come to a close, I feared. From now on, I had to be more like Rose—glamorous and flawless, like I'd been Photoshopped in real life.

I wrinkled my nose at the thought. Crap. I had to fix up before leaving the house—every single time from here on out. Or at least as long as I lasted as duchess. I took the bus back downtown to meet Riggins at the administration building.

Marriage licenses were matters of public record. As soon as we applied for the license, it would be all over the news and social media. I had half a mind to post it myself, but given the situation, it seemed too obvious and self-aggrandizing. Another downside of marrying a titled billionaire—anything I said about it would look like bragging.

If Riggins had just been a regular guy, would I have posted the exciting news on my social media? Absolutely! But if that were the case, we'd be in love and the marriage would be genuine, a real commitment. Not a temporary business arrangement. So maybe it was only hypocrisy that was stopping me from making the announcement.

The administration building was your basic government office building. Hard to find, even though I got off at a stop not far from it. Even still, I almost missed it and walked right by. I had to Google walking directions on my phone and double back. Then I realized there was a bus stop right in front of it. Like, duh. If I'd ridden one stop farther. Nerves, I thought.

I was so anxious, and praying I wasn't late, I barely noticed my surroundings as I stepped inside and looked for the elevator. I had the impression of food, a cafeteria, people eating. But just an impression. My head was elsewhere as I took the elevator to the licensing office.

Riggins was waiting for me as I came off the elevator. His face lit up when he saw me. I almost collapsed with relief. Until that instant, I hadn't thought I'd been worried that he'd be a no-show. Let's just say my insecurities ran deep. He was so hot. So successful. So desired. And I was just me.

So far, so good. No reporters or paparazzi around.

He kissed me lightly. But passionately enough that my heart skipped a beat. It was a natural thing for a groom to do. And smart of him to act the part, in case anyone was looking. But it surprised me nonetheless. And pleased me beyond reason. I was a complete sap.

He took my arm and smiled into my eyes. "You look nervous."

"Oh, really?" I laughed, an embarrassing, girlish titter. I made a note to develop a mature, sophisticated chortle or something more duchesslike in the future. How did duchesses laugh? Or did they just smile patiently at everything?

"That obvious?" I took a deep breath. "This is a big step."

"Not thinking of backing out?" His eyes danced, completely lacking in worry or insecurity. He was clearly teasing.

Looking at him, I knew I would never have the strength to step away from this. No, I *wanted* to marry him. *Way* more than I should have, especially given the circumstances. "Aren't you nervous?"

"Not yet." He took my arm.

I believed him. And wished I had his confidence. I both consoled myself and tortured myself by thinking it was probably easier to be calm when your heart wasn't at stake. When it really was *only* a business transaction to you. A temporary blip in your life.

We got in line. I couldn't help glancing around anxiously, like I expected the press to jump out from behind a potted palm or something.

I eyed the line, looking at the other couples around us. There were some grumpy-looking people, which didn't bode well for the potential longevity of their future marriages at all.

The woman behind me looked as nervous as I was. She seemed to be ignoring her groom behind her. Sensing a sympathetic soul, I turned to her. "Getting a marriage license is nerve-racking, isn't it?"

"I wouldn't know. I'm here getting a license for my dog." She glanced at her watch. "And if they don't hurry, I'm going to have to run out and feed the meter."

Riggins squeezed my hand and stifled a laugh behind his other hand.

"What are you laughing at?" I bumped him playfully. "Did you know this line is also for pet licenses? That's how the county categorizes marriage licenses, as equally important as pet licensing?"

He cupped my chin. "But you are my pet, aren't you, darling? And it makes a certain kind of sense—we're all being collared and put on the choke chain one way or the other."

I rolled my eyes. "Shut up."

He laughed again. "You'll also notice we're in line with a lot of irritated people paying their property taxes." He juggled his hands as if he was weighing something. "Pet licenses, property taxes, getting married—why not lump them all together?"

The woman in front of us turned around and smiled. "If you wanted a dedicated marriage-license-only window, you should have gone to Kent and the Regional Justice Center for your license. They do them separately there." She studied us and frowned slightly, like we looked familiar and she was trying to place us.

My heart stood still. Until she said, "You're such a gorgeous couple!" It was her turn at the counter. "Good luck to you!"

When it was our turn, the clerk handed us an application to fill out and told us to skip the line and bring it back to the window when we finished. We sat next to each other on a hard bench.

"Are you afraid we'll be caught?" I whispered to Riggins.

"We'll almost certainly be found out sooner or later."

I bit my lip and turned my attention to my form. My hand shook as I filled it out. Riggins' hand seemed steady. I stole a peek at his form as he filled in his social security number.

This sounded really dumb, but at that moment I realized that divorce or not, child or not, we would be irrevocably linked forever whether we wanted to be or not. I would know the intimate details of his life, like his social security number, forever. Or until my memory failed. Whichever came first. And he would know mine. Think of the damage I could do with that knowledge. If I were the evil type, of course.

Back at the clerk's station, Riggins paid the license fee in cash. I had another heart-stopping moment when the clerk looked over the form to make sure we'd filled everything in properly. I couldn't imagine she'd miss who Riggins was.

"You must love this job," I said to distract her.

She glanced up at me with a quizzical expression.

"Seeing all the couples getting married—isn't that fun? Wondering what they see in each other and how they chose each other. How they met. It's a fascinating people-study opportunity."

Her face lit up. She chatted for a minute about how nice, in fact, that was. She didn't always get to work marriage licenses. Sometimes she had to work the property-tax-only line. And that was no fun at all.

She finished her job and handed us our license. "Congratulations and best wishes! You look so happy together. So perfect." She leaned forward and lowered her voice. "You're going to be part of the fifty percent of marriages that make it. I have a sense about these things. I'm rarely wrong."

She couldn't know how wrong she was or how much false hope she'd just given me.

As we walked away from the counter, Riggins whispered in my ear, "Nice work distracting her back there."

"I think we got lucky not being recognized." Yes, sometimes I was too modest.

We'd each managed to sneak into the building separately rather well. But leaving the building, we weren't so lucky. Reporters and paparazzi evidently liked to hover around the administration building looking for juicy stories. Or maybe, more likely, someone had recognized us and tipped them off. They followed Riggins around all the time anyway, just for sport. He'd managed to ditch his tail on the way to the admin building, but they'd caught up to him somehow. However they managed to find us, they had.

As we walked out of the building, cameras flashed around us. Riggins grabbed my hand and shielded his eyes with the other. I was grinning, stupidly happy. I probably *should* have tried to mask my feelings, but I simply couldn't. Oh, well. It sold our act. If only Riggins never saw it, I'd be fine.

"Riggins! Riggins!" one of the guys shouted at him. "What were you doing here?" He glanced at me. "With one of the duchess contenders. You chose the American! You applied for a marriage license, admit it! When's the big day?"

"How do you know we haven't just bought a puppy together and come for a license?" Riggins laughed and hustled us into a waiting car.

"It has to be within sixty days! The license is only good for sixty days. We'll find out." The reporter clearly wasn't buying the puppy story. "Why the rush? Didn't you meet less than two weeks ago? Is there something we should know?"

The driver shut the car door, muffling the rest of the reporters' questions.

Riggins squeezed my hand. "Let the games begin."

I smiled shakily and told him about Sally's offer to make the cake. "How many guests *are* we expecting?"

That evening, we made all the national entertainment shows. Sid, Liz, Jasmine, and I huddled in front of the TV with a bowl of popcorn to watch the media circus.

"The Americans have won another battle against the British Empire. Haley Hamilton, the American descendent of the late Most Noble Helen Annette Duchess of Witham, has secured the new Duke of Witham's offer of his hand in marriage after what was reportedly a weekend away at Wareswood Castle with both contenders for the title in attendance and engaged in battle for the duke's attentions.

"Tonight there are thousands upon thousands of disappointed young women on both sides of the pond as their duchess dreams come to an end with the announcement of his engagement made by the duke's PR team late this afternoon. The new duke and his bride-to-be were caught coming out of the King County administration building around four Pacific Time this afternoon.

"Speculation about when and where the wedding will take place has been running high. The duke is keeping the details of his impending nuptials quiet. But we do know that according to Washington State law, the license is only good for sixty days.

"Lady Rose, the other rumored candidate for the job, was unavailable for immediate comment. But she tweeted that she was very happy for the couple and looks forward to being counted among their close acquaintances and helping her American relative adjust to being part of the modern British aristocracy.

"On another of her social media accounts, Lady Rose said, 'I have no doubt cousin Haley will be a most gracious, kind duchess.'

"How's that for being a gracious, classy loser? It's enough to make us almost wish Lady Rose had won the title..."

Our house was surrounded by reporters waiting to snap our picture and trying to interview us. Riggins once again sent his security team over to keep them and other curiosity seekers at a safe distance. Our poor neighborhood was overrun. I felt sorry for our neighbors and was apologetic about the inconvenience. And worried about Sid, Jasmine, and Liz. Would all this die down after the wedding? Or had I inadvertently destroyed the privacy of their lives, too?

The rest of the week passed in a blur of wedding planning, dress fittings, meetings with lawyers, and signings of prenups.

Mr. Thorne met with me privately and handed me a generous advance from the estate. "For the bride's share of the wedding expenses, as instructed by the late duke. He wanted his heir to have a wedding befitting of his status, even if the wedding was small and put together quickly. The late duke realized the necessary wedding would be out of your budget."

Maybe I should have been insulted, but I took the money without too many scruples. Why shouldn't the Dead Duke pay?

I panicked on Friday when I realized I didn't have a ring for Riggins. How was I even going to afford one? Especially one good enough for a duke and a billionaire?

I called Kayla.

"Calm down. Don't worry. I'll refer you to our favorite jewelry store. Make a private appointment and take Riggins with you. Let him pick his ring and get it sized."

"But the cost—"

"In cases like these, it's traditional for him to pay for his own. He knows your budget is limited, when his is basically unlimited."

"But I can't—"

"You can. And if you won't, you can always take a loan out from Riggins and pay it back when you come into your inheritance. Your late great-aunt left you something, didn't she?"

I took a deep breath. "Yes." Several hundred million. Once I produced an heir. Like that was going to happen.

"Okay, then. There you go."

But I wasn't satisfied with letting Riggins pay. I called Mr. Thorne. "I need an advance on my money. Enough to buy Riggins a wedding band."

Mr. Thorne laughed. "You've used all the wedding money already?"

"No, of course not. I want to buy Riggins a ring with *my* money, not the Dead Duke's. Can you get some for me?"

I could hear the smile in Mr. Thorne's voice. "Your request sounds fair enough to me. I'll see what I can do."

So less than twenty-four hours before my wedding, and just a few hours before our rehearsal dinner, we met at the jewelry store and picked out a simple platinum band for Riggins. And I paid for it with an advance on my settlement for producing an heir. Was I getting in too deep? Being too prideful? Maybe. But I didn't care.

I was deliriously happy. Happier than I ever remembered being and determined to live in the moment. A month from now, a year, maybe, this fairytale would all be over. For now I had to enjoy it and worry about replacing the money later.

I'd worry about everything later. Later, after Sid was cured.

CHAPTER FOUR

H *aley*
　　I'd passed the test—the non-pregnancy test, anyway. The wedding was on.

Dressed in a strapless organza, hand-beaded, dropped waist, lace ball gown that cost more than I made in a year, I stood in front of the floor-to-ceiling plate glass windows of Riggins' waterfront mansion, staring into his eyes, pledging my troth. A sash was tied at my waist, pinned with a large, beautiful organza flower. I was so nervous, I felt like it was breaking me in half. My world was splintering into my regular life before Riggins and my extraordinary life after marrying him. From obscure to under the spotlight.

I was in the middle of my transformation from commoner to duchess. From single maiden to married matron. From honest person to world-class liar. What do you call a woman who marries strictly for business? Kept? Or was that only for mistresses?

And was I really that woman, even though my motives were pure?

I had insisted on being married by a layman. I wasn't particularly religious, but that wasn't why. Something about vowing to remain married until death do us part before God and a clergyman, when I knew for certain we'd soon be divorcing, seemed too hypocritical and reckless. Sacrilegious. Like courting disaster. It was bad enough I was pledging it in front of friends and family. And so we were being married by a justice of the peace Riggins found for the occasion. God's laws may be immutable, but the law of the land was fluid and subject to interpretation. I felt more comfortable bending it and lying to it.

Because my father was dead, Mr. Thorne gave me away. Which somehow seemed both appropriate and wildly funny. Like the devil handing me out of a car into the underworld. Whatever happened, I wasn't coming out of this marriage unscathed and innocent.

My heart squeezed and ached. My breath caught as I looked into Riggins' dark, snapping eyes, and placed my cold hands into his warm ones. My mouth was dry. My voice shook as I repeated my vows. His was calm, deep, in control. It didn't waver, not once.

"Do you take this woman to be your lawfully wedded wife?" the justice said in a sonorous voice.

"I do."

"Rings?"

And then Riggins was sliding Helen's matching antique wedding band onto my finger next to her...my...engagement ring. Which I'd barely had a chance to get used to wearing, and now it was being joined by its mate.

Riggins looked deep into my eyes and repeated a standard set of vows we'd found on the Internet. "With this ring, I marry you:

With my loving heart.

With my willing body.

And with my eternal soul."

You'd think he would have choked on the words, instead of sounding so sincere he nearly broke my heart. Eternal soul? Really? I'd begged him to simply leave it at "With this ring, I marry you." He'd argued that wouldn't look right. Not romantic or fairytale enough. That it wouldn't sell this passionate whirlwind romance to the world, and certainly not to our small audience. That it would cause suspicion and gossip right away. Even though a decent number of people attending knew the truth.

We couldn't find a set of ring exchange vows that didn't mention love in one form or another. And he refused the antiquated "With this ring, I thee wed," claiming we weren't living in King James' England. Not yet, anyway.

Then it was my turn to slip the platinum band on his finger. To look into his eyes and say words that I meant, but that would never be true. "With this ring, I marry you:

With my loving heart.

With my willing body.

And with my eternal soul."

"I now pronounce you man and wife," the justice said. "You may kiss the bride."

I gave my new husband a shaky smile. I was marrying, no, married to, the hottest guy I'd ever known. Charming. Smart. Funny. Rich. He had my heart. But he didn't want it. At least not long term.

I closed my eyes, wondering what kind of kiss he meant to give me. A little peck? Or something to remember this moment by?

He wrapped his arms around me and pulled me close, crushing me against the stiffness of his shirt, so close I inhaled the heady, expensive scent of his cologne. I wrapped my arms around his neck. As our lips met, I felt the usual, but still surprising, jolt. The total awareness of him. The melding. His lips were hard and insistent against mine. I had my answer. This might have only been a performance, but we were going to give our audience something to talk about.

His kiss lingered. His lips were warm and moist. I leaned into him and pressed my kiss to his with more passion than was strictly polite. I wished I could stay in his arms forever. But soon the piper would be paid. We pulled back, smiling into each other's eyes.

"Ladies and gentlemen—the Duke and Duchess of Witham!"

And just that quickly, I was no longer Haley Marie Hamilton. I was no longer a person with a real last name at all. I wasn't simply Mrs. Feldhem. I was Her

Grace, or ma'am, or duchess. On formal legal papers, Most Noble Haley Marie Duchess of Witham.

"The duke and duchess invite you all to eat, drink, and be merry. Please enjoy the buffet."

Sid had tears in her eyes as she hugged me, and then Riggins.

The evening was only beginning. I had no idea what Riggins had planned for our wedding night. He'd been secretive about it. What would my billionaire groom surprise me with? Would we jet off somewhere on a private plane? My heart pounded with both anxiety and anticipation at the thought of the pleasures of the night ahead.

Somehow I made it through dinner: the endless toasts, the ribbing, the cake cutting of the beautiful concoction Sally and her team had made, and conversation after conversation. Finally, it was getting late. The guests were getting restless. You know how it is when you're trying to hang on until the bride and groom leave and they just keep hanging out like they'll never go, and you want to go home and put your feet up. Were all the guests spending the night? Were we spending the night at the mansion, too? Was this going to be an all-night affair?

Riggins took my hand. "Not to look *too* eager, but it *is* my wedding night." He smiled at me. "And we have important business to attend to." He pulled me to the full-length glass back patio doors.

As if on cue, a row of trees lit up, decorated with strings and strings of white lights and hanging lanterns, lighting a path across the lawn to the dock. At the end of the dock, Riggins' yacht lit up. In the brilliance of its fully lit splendor, I could see the back railing strung with roses and flowers that matched my bouquet.

A crew member dressed in white waited to welcome us aboard, putting down the gangplank decorated with a red carpet.

Sid handed me my bouquet, her eyes sparkling with tears of happiness. "You'll need this." She hugged me suddenly, fiercely. "I'm so happy for you."

I hugged her back. "I'm happy for us." She knew whom I meant—her and me.

Riggins was momentarily distracted by one of the guests.

"I hope you didn't do this just for me," Sid whispered softly so Riggins couldn't hear. "You look too happy for that."

"Nothing would make me happier than you being cured," I whispered back.

"But the way you look at him..." She searched my face. "Don't lose him, Hale. Do whatever you have to hang on to him. For your sake."

I laughed softly. "What kind of wedding talk is this?" I paused. "As soon as you're out of school for summer, you'll have to come to Witham House with me. Sound fun?"

She grinned. "Riggins said you're to throw your bouquet from the bow of the yacht before you pull out."

Lazer came up beside us. "Who's pulling out? Not him, I hope." He hitched his thumb toward Riggins.

Riggins' attention came back on us. He rolled his eyes. "Come, duchess. Your vessel awaits."

"Shouldn't that be vassal, Your Grace?" Justin slapped him on the back.

"I'm never going to hear the end of this." Riggins grinned.

A pianist and harp had been playing all evening. They started on a melodic Bach processional. The crowd gathered around us. A pair of waiters dressed in tails opened the patio doors with great fanfare. All we needed was a trumpet to make the atmosphere complete.

"My lady." Riggins grinned at me again and led me through the doors and down the path as our guests followed us.

Along the path on Riggins' arm. Onto the dock. To the ship. Where only Riggins and I mounted the gangplank and boarded the vessel and our guests congregated on the dock, as the crew pulled up the gangplank and prepared for departure.

On the dock, a group of all the single women formed. As the yacht's engine fired up and the staff removed the tethers, I leaned over the rail and tossed my bouquet directly to Sid. Rose, who'd been well behaved all evening—I'd hoped she would have the good grace to make her excuses not to attend, but she hadn't—made a lunge for it. Sid caught it anyway and beamed at me, completely ignoring Rose.

I turned to Riggins and lifted my skirt. "Aren't you going to snap the garter?"

He laughed. "To that crowd? There aren't many single guys there."

I laughed and raised an eyebrow. "There are at least two who need it badly. What about Lazer? And your lawyer Harry?"

"Toss it! Toss it! Toss it!" people began chanting. I put my foot up on the rail. Riggins grabbed my thigh, sending a spark of desire through me, and removed the garter. The boat had already begun pulling away when he snapped it like a pro directly at Lazer. It hit Lazer dead center in the middle of his chest. If it had been a bullet, he'd have been dead. Lazer caught it automatically, realizing a second too late what he'd done and making a comical face of disgust. Justin was slapping him on the back, ribbing him, you could tell, as the yacht pulled away.

Riggins and I waved from the railing as the boat pulled away into Lake Washington. When we were a respectable distance away, he took my hand and pulled me across the deck, up the stairs, and inside the boat.

"I've been wanting to show you the master suite since our first date here." His eyes sparkled. His voice was husky.

I hoped he wasn't teasing. Because if that was the case, if he wanted me the way I wanted him, maybe...

My heart pounded so loudly in my ears it was nearly deafening. I wanted him. But I wanted *all* of him—heart, mind, body, and soul. But I wasn't likely to get more than his body. Maybe that was enough for now. But I ached with desire for his vows to me to be true.

He showed me into the hallway and scooped me up beneath the knees to carry me over the threshold of the master suite, closing the doors behind him.

The room was as magnificent as anything in his mansion, and echoed its style. It sat on the top deck of the boat. One side of the suite was all windows, like his mansion. Outside, the moon shone and the stars and city lights twinkled in the distance across the black lake.

The bed sat on a round platform, raised in importance, and surrounded by sleek white columns like an altar to some pagan god. The bed was turned down and spread with red rose petals. A floor-to-ceiling mirror decorated the wall next to the bed. There was a huge, round window, skylight, whatever, over the bed, so large it was almost the size of the bed. A porthole to the sky.

A bottle of wine chilled in an ice bucket on a small, round table near the windows, which had a built-in window seat covered in sleek red leather. A plate of chocolates, cheese, and other nibbles were on the table. There were built-in cabinets and closets all in rich, glossy woods with warm, romantic red tones. Candles flickered on the bedside tables in silver candlestick holders.

The room was as breathtaking and sexy as its owner. No detail had been spared. It felt like I had stepped into a romantic fairytale, a dream world I would wake up from any moment. I couldn't have imagined a more perfect setting.

Riggins turned to me. "Do you like it?"

"Like it? How can you even ask? I'm overwhelmed
with its beauty." And masculinity. "I feel shabby in
comparison."

He lifted my chin and stared into my eyes. "You
don't look the least bit shabby, duchess. Anything but."
My heart trilled. It was the perfect time to confess
his undying love for me, even if it was a lie. Anything to
soothe my vanity. But he didn't, and I'd have to live
with that.

He took my hand in his large, warm one and led me
to the window seat, where he sat me down gently. "You
must be tired of standing in these heels."

He kneeled before me like a white knight, slid my
shoes off, and massaged my feet through my white
stockings until I sighed softly and moaned with almost
sexual pleasure. If this was the beginning of his seduc-
tion, he was very good indeed.

We'd just come from a full buffet dinner, but I'd
eaten very little. Not much more than the delicate bite
of cake he'd fed me. I'd left half a dozen untouched
plates here and there around the reception. I'd been too
nervous. Too busy playing hostess. Too much the main
attraction. Trying too hard to be calm and elegant. I
still wasn't particularly hungry, but I was thirsty. I
needed something to settle my nerves and ease my conscience.

I'd never really imagined going to my wedding night
a virgin. But I *had* imagined my husband being in love
with me. Desperately so, if at all possible. Now I needed
some liquid courage to get over the shattering of my
girlish dreams and the embarrassment and shyness I

suddenly felt. We'd never even seen each other naked. I glanced at the ice bucket with longing.

Riggins caught my look. "Thirsty? Should I pop the cork?"

I bit my lip. "You wouldn't happen to have anything stronger, would you? Something smooth and fast-acting?"

"Nervous?"

"Is it that obvious?" I looked at him with an open appeal to reassure me.

He smiled encouragingly. "When you ask for a drink like that? Yeah. It's a dead giveaway." He laughed softly. "Want to know a secret? So am I. I've never deflowered a virgin before. Introducing a woman to the sensual pleasures is a grave responsibility."

I laughed and shook my head. "You're making fun."

"I'm being honest. I'm serious." He looked anything but.

Even though I didn't believe him, my breath caught. "You don't have to worry about that. Or corrupting me. Just because I'm *technically* a virgin doesn't mean I don't know *anything*."

He grinned. "That takes the pressure off. Somewhat." He got up, opened a cupboard, and pulled out a bottle of expensive, aged Scotch. "I was saving this for a special occasion. I guess getting married counts." He poured two glasses and came back to hand one to me.

I caught the glint of his wedding band, looking so new and shiny on his finger. I had to resist the wonder and swelling pride. This man was mine, *my* husband. At least for the duration.

I tossed my drink back quickly with a smooth flick of my wrist, feeling the smooth burn. I set my glass down beside me and leaned back, studying him. If he was horrified I'd just chugged that Scotch and not savored it, he kept it to himself as he coolly enjoyed his glass.

"So where are we going?" I tried to sound casual. "Are we cruising to anyplace specific? Or just cruising?"

"I've instructed the captain to take us to the ocean for sunrise. We'll cruise the lake, go through the cut, into the sound, and through the Strait of Juan de Fuca to the Pacific."

"Sounds romantic." I smiled at him.

"It should be. If the sunrise cooperates."

"And after that?"

"Back to Seattle to catch a private flight to England. I promised you a honeymoon in our castle."

I nodded. "Yes, the castle." I took a deep breath. "I've looked it up online. There are many pictures of the interior. But the outside is kind of intimidating."

He laughed. "We'll face it together. I've looked it up, too. The Dead Duke didn't post many current pictures. I hope Thorne isn't lying about the fabulous restoration the Dead Duke did during his lifetime. He supposedly put a two-hundred-year roof on the place."

He shook his head. "Can you imagine? Here, I think a fifty-year-roof is pretty much top of the line. At least we shouldn't have to replace it in our lifetime. Thorne said that was the point. The Dead Duke didn't trust his heir, specifically me, to keep the place up. That's my

take. Thorne says the Dead Duke was just being cour-
teous by taking care of all those boring, yet expensive,
home maintenance projects during his lifetime."

We fell silent.

I screwed up my courage. "Can I ask you something?"

"Anything." He swirled the Scotch in his glass.

"Why *did* you marry me?"

He continued to study me, amused. "You know the
answer to that. The Dead Duke forced my hand."

"No, I mean, why *me* and not Rose? If you're not in
love with either of us, she seems so much more perfect
for the role. I never thought—"

He pressed a finger to my lips. "You asked me not to
tell you, remember? Are you asking me to break my
promise now?"

"I asked you not to tell me the results of the DNA
test. That's not the same thing." I hoped. But I was
fishing, wasn't I? That was ill-mannered of me. He
could have easily said he married me because Rose
turned out not to be related to the late duchess. Would
that have soothed my vanity or not?

He caught my cheek and looked me deeply in the
eyes so penetratingly it was as if he could see straight
into my soul. "Maybe I just wanted you more than I
wanted her. Maybe I burned for you." His tone was
light and teasing as he ran his fingers gently over my
chest, sliding them lightly over the cleft between my
breasts.

"Burning is better than nothing," I said.

"If you're going to be forced into marriage, it helps." He was still teasing, but his tone was laced with desire and his eyes had gone dark.

I laughed nervously, afraid to put too much stock in what he was saying, and ran the backs of my fingers over the five o'clock stubble on his chin. The Scotch had settled pleasantly over me, making me bold. "Mr. Thorne reiterated to me before the ceremony that there was to be no funny business. No faking this marriage. We're to consummate it quickly. On our wedding night. It has to be absolutely legal."

"Quickly? Where's the fun in that?" Riggins looked surprised and amused. "He used the words 'funny business'?"

I shrugged. "I may have taken a little liberty with his exact phrasing."

"He gave me the same instructions." Riggins pulled me to my feet.

"At least he's consistent." I braced my hands against his chest and untied his tie as he slipped out of his jacket and tossed it away in a move I found completely sexy.

He bent and kissed the tops of my breasts where they peeked out of my gown. I stared at the top of his dark head, wanting to press his head down and beg him to lick and kiss as he pleased.

I was corseted in and my breasts were shoved up, which made me more breathless than usual. His touch set me on fire. An ache of need began building between my legs. Soon I'd be slick and ready for him, virgin or no.

The hairdresser had pinned my hair up in an elaborate knot. Riggins pulled the pins out one by one until my hair fell loose around my shoulders.

"Beautiful," he whispered as he ran his fingers through it and kissed my shoulders almost reverently. He was being very gentle, treating me like fine porcelain when I was really nothing more than common earthenware. I assumed my virginity really did have him spooked.

If he *meant* to kill me with tenderness and romantic gestures and by drawing out the inevitable, he was doing a damn good job of it. My nipples budded into tight raspberries, tighter than I ever remembered, physically aching for his touch.

I forced myself not to breathe too quickly or shallowly, not easy given how excited I was, and turned and lifted my hair off my neck. "Let's get on with the legalities, shall we? I need help getting out of this dress. It took Sid ten minutes to button me in. Will you do the honors and unbutton me?"

He fumbled over the first few. I bit my lip to keep from laughing at his attempts and the sweet thought that he really was nervous.

After a few attempts, he got the hang of pulling the silk loops over the slick silk buttons. His fingers glided down my back until my dress fell open in the back and I felt the coolness of the room.

I stepped out of the dress and draped it over a nearby chair. It was too beautiful and expensive to leave on the floor. I had to keep going before I lost my nerve. I turned to face him and reached for the buttons of his shirt.

"Cuffs first." He held his arm out to me.

I unbuttoned one, then the other, feeling his pulse, strong and rapid, as I ran my hand over his inner wrists. I liked to imagine his pulse raced for me, not just at the thought of sex. I unbuttoned his shirt and slid it off over his shoulders, running my hands over the firm planes, and letting his shirt fall at his feet.

His chest was firm and well defined. Beautiful to look at and stroke. I wanted to turn things around. Show him he shouldn't be afraid of me, or of hurting me. That I wasn't made of glass. Prove to him he hadn't been wrong to pick the less experienced woman or to worry about my virginity.

The corset shoved my breasts up to the point that my nipples very nearly popped out. I was trying not to breathe hard and emphasize them. But I was excited as I leaned forward and took his nipple in my mouth, running my tongue around it, and sucking as he cupped his hand around the back of my head and laced his fingers through my hair.

I felt him kiss the top of my head. He whispered something to himself.

Without warning, he released my head and pulled me away from him. His eyes were very dark now, his pupils large with arousal. My heart pounded rapidly despite my best efforts to slow it.

"Fair's fair." He spun me around so that my back was toward him.

He kissed my neck as he untied the strings that held me in and unlaced my corset until it was loose enough for me to step out of. He tossed it away then slowly turned me around to face him.

I stood before him in my white lace thong panties decorated with a tiny blue ribbon, my thigh-high white nylons, and nothing else. My breasts budded even tighter beneath his gaze. The way he stared at me, and them, took my breath away. When he bent and sucked them, I went weak at the knees.

I reached for the hook at his pants. Released it. Slid his zipper down, and then his pants. He stepped out of them, still sucking on my breasts and using his tongue like an expert. I kissed the top of his head and helped him out of his boxers. He was erect and hard, totally delicious.

He finally released my breast and kissed me, hard and insistently, his tongue dancing with mine. I pulled away and kissed his neck. His shoulder. I slid kisses down his chest, nibbling and gently biting. I sucked his nipples, hard. Bit them just to the edge of pain. Then fell to my knees, intent on taking him in my mouth.

He caught me and pulled me to my feet before I could take him, swept me into his arms and carried me to the bed, laying me on my back and perching over me, staring at me with the most intense look. In stark contrast to my roughness, he bent and kissed me gently, very sweetly. Romantically.

He kissed my neck. I sighed softly and guided his kisses toward my breasts again. They ached for him. I ached for him.

He kissed me between my breasts. Then slid lower. Almost before I realized what he was doing, he slid my panties off, pressed my legs apart, and buried his face between my legs, sucking and kissing my sweet spot until I threatened to come.

"No," I whispered, begging him to stop, not wanting the release until he was inside.

Suddenly, he pulled away and perched over me again. "You're so fucking beautiful."

Ah, the art of distraction. As my heart sang beneath his appreciation and sense of wonder, he slid into me with a single, hard thrust.

I gasped, surprised by the sudden pain. I was so ready for him, and yet...

I whimpered.

"You're so tight. So wonderfully tight." The sense of awe in his voice made my heart sing as the cleft between my legs reacted to the intrusion and fullness of him.

I whimpered again.

He kissed me, silencing me as he thrust deeper into me. "Wrap your legs around me," he whispered in a husky voice I barely recognized.

If that was what he wanted, who was I to argue? I wrapped my legs around the taut muscles of his back, digging my heels in and rising up to meet him. Looking him in the eye.

Overhead, stars sparkled through our candlelight reflection in the big, round window above the bed. It was almost mirrorlike in quality. We looked ethereal. Ghostly. See-through. Otherworldly. Particularly me in my white hosiery with my silvery hair fanned out on the pillow. We looked as if we were erotic lovers placed in the sky next to the W of Cassiopeia, the vain queen who boasted of her beauty. I wasn't vain, but as I watched the reflected muscles in Riggins' back tense, my legs wrapped around him, locking him tight as he took me, I thought we were beautiful. The act *was* beautiful.

"Like what you see, duchess?" Riggins whispered.

I blushed. *Caught.* I looked him in the eye to explain.

He thrust again, cutting off any response I could make. And again. Deeper and deeper as I held his gaze. He was daring me, looking for something, but I had no idea what.

The pain melted into pleasure. I gasped and closed my eyes as the fever pitch built. I clasped him tightly as the waves built. Finally, I let myself go and surrendered to the pleasure. As I cried out in completion, he covered my mouth with his, kissing me deeply. He grunted and gave a final deep thrust, still kissing me. I felt a oneness with him that was almost frightening as the waves of pleasure kept crashing.

When he finally released my mouth, he brushed my hair out of my face tenderly. "I hope I didn't hurt you."

"You nearly killed me." I was completely breathless.

His eyes went large.

"With pleasure. That was...exquisite." I smiled, so full of joy it was scary. "Can you say that about sex?"

"You just did." He looked incredibly pleased. He was still inside me. And still *very* large. Like, huge.

I swore I felt every inch of him. And that he'd just opened me to everything carnal and wonderful. Later, I imagined I'd appreciate him being so well hung. But at this particular moment...

I smiled, trying not to laugh and not to cry. I was weak with emotion. "I hope you won't take this the wrong way, but would you mind pulling out?"

He smiled back. "A little too much man for you, am I?"

"Oh, shut up." I shoved him playfully. "I'm a virgin. You can only expect so much at once."

"*Were*. You *were* a virgin. I just made a real woman out of you. And Thorne is very relieved."

He was so clearly teasing, I couldn't help laughing. "Out. Please?"

"Polite to the end. I'm going to have to teach you how to talk dirty." He pulled out and collapsed beside me, staring at me. "Cold?" He grinned again and pulled the covers up.

As he did, he sent a bunch of rose petals flying. One landed on my nose, another on my cheek, a third on my lips. I blew it away and sneezed.

"Damn, when people say life's no bed of roses, they have no idea what they're saying." He laughed and brushed the petals away.

He pulled me close. "At least we fit well together."

"When you first entered me, I had my doubts," I said. "It felt like you were tearing me in two."

"That bad?" He winced. "I thought I was being gentle."

I laughed at his shocked expression. "As awful as it sounds, it was wonderful at the same time." I sighed happily. "Even though you're out, I can still feel you. It's like my body's still reacting to you."

It was true. I was pleasantly achy. The muscles of my vagina were still contracting.

We lay side by side on the bed and looked up at ourselves and the stars above us.

"That's a very naughty window you have, duke." I raised an eyebrow.

"Is it? I like to consider it nautical. What do you have against stargazing?" His eyes danced.

"Mirrors by the bed. A highly reflective window above it. Do you always watch yourself perform?" I asked.

"I didn't see a thing. The stars are for your pleasure, the pleasure of the person on the bottom."

I blushed again.

As he studied me and the stars overhead, I felt him go hard again against my leg. And the sheets were getting a rise out of something.

I pointed overhead to the reflection of the tented sheet in the window above. "Is that the Milky Way?"

"Stop teasing, duchess." He stroked my thigh and looked at me for permission.

"Again?"

"Once a night is never enough..."

I smiled and tugged him playfully on top of me.

You only get one wedding night. And one deflowering in your life, period. I might as well enjoy the pain. It was, as I'd said, exquisite.

"Hard and fast, Riggins," I whispered.

CHAPTER FIVE

*H*aley "How are we going to get to Witham House from the airport?" I'd asked Riggins on the flight over. He'd been so mysterious about everything honeymoon.

"Buy a car when we arrive? Maybe a Bentley, like Lazer's?" I'd joked, as I had been about most things billionaire. Having money to throw away made me feel guilty when others had so little. I was still fresh from the struggle of trying to keep Sid and me afloat amid her medical bills and college costs. I continued having a hard time with the concept of being filthy rich. And the filthy part was winning and weighing on my conscience. "Only with the steering wheel on the other

side, because this is England, after all. If Lazer can buy
a car for the weekend—"

"Damn Lazer. I'm not playing keep-up with Lazer."
He grinned, clearly not angry. "And why should we buy
a Bentley when we have a fleet of luxury vehicles the
Dead Duke left us? His driver will meet us at the airport and drive us to Witham House."

"A fleet?" I laughed and put on a fake pout. "But
those are all *used* cars. I want a *new* one!"

"Oh, my little pampered duchess. Feeling entitled
already?" He kissed me, silencing my protest that I was
only joking. He knew that.

Riggins' friendship with Lazer was puzzling. I'd
given up trying to figure it out. But clearly, it was a hot
point.

I couldn't help teasing Riggins. And flirting with
him at every opportunity. There was an easy intimacy
between us now, the familiarity of lovers. Whenever we
looked at each other, we grinned. Just like real in-love
newlyweds. I knew why I was grinning like that. But
Riggins?

I didn't want to get my hopes up. He still hadn't
professed his love to me, not even after lovemaking.
Which was customary, right? Even if you didn't mean
it. Still, I appreciated his honesty. If he ever *did* say he
loved me, I'd have to assume he meant it.

At least we had lust to keep us together. I'd never
really been worried that we didn't have chemistry. It
was there in the air between us from the beginning,
whether he wanted to deny it or not. But I was still
pleasantly surprised by the depth and intensity of the

passion that drew us together. And the longing that made us want to couple as often as possible. And the reaction of our bodies to each other.

I might have chalked up my reaction to him as my inexperience and naivety, but there was no denying he wanted me, too. As much, or more, as I wanted him. He just didn't have the accompanying soreness to slow him down.

We'd been married just over twenty-four hours and had already made love so often I was in danger of losing count, and each time was something special. Wasn't the world wonderful when everything was a first?

The morning after, on our first full day of marriage, Riggins woke me to the sun rising over the Pacific Ocean. No small feat, since the Pacific was to the west of land. But he'd had the captain speed through the Strait of Juan de Fuca overnight and cruise far enough out into the ocean that the curvature of the earth made land invisible so the sun would rise over the water.

He'd opened the blinds so we could watch the sun rise from bed. And made sure none of the crew came up on our deck. Yes, I was modest. I didn't want anyone walking in on us, or past us on the deck, which in my book was the same as, while we made love.

Simple pleasures, though. It didn't take much to thrill and titillate me. I didn't need handcuffs or chains. The open curtains were dangerous enough to make sex even more exciting. Though with Riggins, sex was inherently exhilarating.

As if making love to an ocean sunrise wasn't unique enough, he'd also initiated me into the mile-high club on the chartered plane to England. The bedroom suite hadn't been as sumptuous as his master suite on the yacht, but the thrill had been the same. We even made love with the plane window shade up. Though that, obviously, didn't have the same thrill as open curtains on a yacht.

Now I was looking forward to making love in a private castle.

The driver met us as promised. It was all very discreet. We were trying to avoid the press, after all. I wasn't probably the most popular person, being the American winner. To the British way of thinking, there were too few coveted duchess positions that came on the market for one of them to go to an American commoner. It wasn't even like I could strongly disagree with their point of view. We also had our new station to think about.

The driver greeted us with the reverence reserved for our status, loaded our bags into the car, and we were off to the several thousand acres we owned in the countryside outside of London somewhere. Geography wasn't my best subject.

I had never been to England, Great Britain, the United Kingdom, whatever it was that I should have been calling it. As an American, all the names confused me. Though I knew enough that England was one country, Scotland another in the kingdom, etc. Crazy to be a duchess in a land you've never been to and whose customs, and even geography, were foreign to you.

Riggins had been several times. On the flight over we'd looked at the portfolio of pictures Mr. Thorne had given us of the castle, and read about the history. I was already intimidated, to say the least. I just couldn't believe a single family could own such magnificence.

Just like Wareswood, the entrance to the estate was gated. You didn't want any old riffraff to get in. Not easily, anyway. And certainly no poachers. Though poaching was no longer the capital offense it had been in the Middle Ages, Mr. Thorne said we still had a gamekeeper who was on the lookout for that kind of thing. The game on the estate must be carefully managed if we were to have a healthy ecosystem. Poaching threw it off balance.

The driver buzzed in through the gate at the entrance of the estate by texting someone at the house. The drive through the woods and park was longer than I'd imagined.

I turned to Riggins. "How many thousand acres do you own?"

"Three." He smiled.

"What does that translate to in miles?" I couldn't help grinning.

"I have no idea."

"Are we almost there?" I bumped him playfully. "I can't believe you own all the eye can see, Your Grace." I carefully avoided saying "we" owned it. Because I didn't.

We rounded a gentle corner. The castle came into view on the hill before us. It was a castle in every sense, complete with fortified stone walls, a castle keep, the remains of a moat, and turreted towers.

The history Mr. Thorne had given us said there was even a dungeon. As well as a chapel. A ghost tower, aptly, and with a flair for the obvious, named the Ghost Tower, which you could be pretty sure I wasn't venturing into. Well, of course after seven hundred years and all of its history, the castle would be haunted. As long as the haunting was confined to one tower...

Maybe we could get Lazer to come with his ghost-hunting equipment and evict it.

And there were all manner of gardens, including a Victorian garden and a separate poison garden, which intrigued me. Not that I had any intention of poisoning anyone, but it sounded mysterious and very gothic.

The day was sunny, thank goodness. In the gray of a typical rainy English day, the thing would have been absolutely foreboding and terrifying. I could imagine someone like poor Jane Eyre coming to a place like this to work.

"Wow!" I said without thinking. Yes, I'd seen pictures, but nothing had really prepared me for the reality.

Riggins was staring at it, too, with a fully business-like expression. Like, *How the hell am I going to run this monstrosity? It's a bloody corporation that needs a fulltime CEO, chief cook, and bottle washer.*

Notice how I even threw a little British into his thoughts. He was learning, and so was I.

Riggins didn't seem particularly pleased by the awesome sight. Which wasn't good for my case to remain the duchess. As long as he fought being the duke—okay, he'd always be the duke until he died, but as long as he fought keeping the estate—I was fighting a losing battle to remain his wife.

After a marriage that could still be counted in hours, I knew that I didn't want anyone else but Riggins for the rest of my life. At the tender age of my early twenties, I didn't want to end up sad and alone, divorced and longing for a man I could never have again. There was way too much of my life ahead of me for that.

He had to fall in love with the place. He *had* to. And then maybe there would be time for him to fall in love with me. Or at least make an heir and multiple spares. And maybe by then be settled into pleasant domesticity together.

Oh, crap. Since when I had aligned myself with the Dead Duke? Sigh.

The medieval castle had been in Riggins' family for over seven hundred years, even when his ancestors had only been earls. Which was unfathomable to an American like me. Our whole country wasn't that old. Not even if you went all the way back to Jamestown.

I leaned over and whispered into Riggins' ear, "How can anyone call *that* a house?"

"It was called Witham Castle until the French Revolution, when the British aristocrats got nervous that French sentiments against the aristocracy might infect British citizens and lead to an off-with-their-heads movement. The Earl of Witham at the time insisted on renaming the castle Witham House so that it sounded more modest."

I rolled my eyes at that harebrained scheme. "On paper, maybe. But if you ever saw it, how could you deny what it was?"

Riggins shrugged. "Hubris. We Feldhems are known for it."

I raised an eyebrow. We broke out laughing.

The car pulled through an arch between two stone towers that must have had a drawbridge at some point. Either that or some badass wooden doors with wrought iron hinges.

I felt totally intimidated, suddenly catching a large dose of Riggins' reluctance to be lord of this place. Seeing it in person, I couldn't imagine really living here and *managing* it. Suddenly I longed for Seattle and my parents' average, middle-class, cozy home. And Sid.

Riggins squeezed my hand as the car swung around the drive and pulled in front of the main entrance. A middle-aged man in tails stood at the bottom of the stairs.

He came out to greet us and opened my car door. As he gave me a hand out, he nearly did a double take, looking almost as if he'd seen a ghost. I was obviously a curiosity to him.

"Gibson, ma'am. I'm your butler."

I wanted to ask him to call me Haley, but restrained myself. We weren't in casual old America anymore.

He regained his composure. "Your Grace," he said to Riggins.

Riggins nodded. "Good to finally meet you in person, Gibson. I appreciate the care you've taken with the place in this interim period between ducal reigns."

"It's my job, sir." But Gibson looked pleased as the driver began to unload our bags. "I've opened and aired the master suite for you and the duchess, as instructed. And set up a day of meetings with individual staff members for tomorrow, sir. I thought you'd want to spend the first day getting settled."

He showed us up the steps to the house and paused at the entrance to let us go through. I was about to step in when Riggins caught me in his arms. "No way, duchess. This is our new home. I have to carry you over the threshold."

"Why, duke!" I said. "You're such a romantic." I was laughing as Riggins caught me beneath the knees and carried me into the castle.

Whatever Gibson thought of the show, he kept it to himself as the driver followed behind with our luggage.

When we stepped into the reception room and Riggins set me down, I gasped again. The great stairway across from us looked like something a king should descend while wearing a red velvet cape trimmed with spotted white fur. I had the impression of white—white stone and granite or something—and great quantities of light shining in through the tall, crowned windows at the top of the landing. A red carpet ran up the middle of the stairs, which looked like they belonged in an elegant institution, not my home. I never thought people actually rolled out the red carpet, or had it permanently installed on their home staircases. The stairs were double, or triple, or quadruple wide, with a railing that looked like an altar at the top. Eyeballing them, it was hard to judge exactly how wide they were. Everything was so enormous in scale. Heavy vases filled with potted plants sat on either side of the altar-looking edifice. Massive plants. Trees, really.

The Dead Duke had spent his hundred-year reign restoring the castle interior to its Italianate Renaissance splendor. Walking in was like stepping into a glorious past century. A time when opulence was expected, status existed to flaunt, and money flowed freely.

Riggins was beside me, very quiet, scarily quiet, as he took in the inner sanctum of his dukedom. I pictured him seeing money flying out the window and a million administrative details plaguing him. Time, time, bloody limited time. Time and effort he needed for Flash being siphoned away.

I was intimidated. Oh yes, very. But crazily, I was also enthralled. Impressed. Almost proud. Taken in by all the exceptional artwork and décor.

"I'll show you to your rooms, sir. You and the duchess will want to freshen up and rest before dinner. I'd be happy to give you a tour of the house at your convenience."

Riggins nodded. "Excellent. Very thoughtful."

We followed Gibson up the stairs and down a long corridor where pictures of Riggins' ancestors from over the centuries hung. I didn't see any recent enough to be the Dead Duke. I assumed his portrait must be displayed somewhere more prominent.

I remembered Riggins' aversion to just such a display. But I felt a kinship with them that seemed lost on him. Secretly, I was hoping to see a portrait of Helen hanging here. Because, very vainly, it would almost be like having a picture of me in the place, putting my mark on it. The more permanent a fixture I became...

I made a mental note to go on a long exploration and see if any of her touches were still around and if any more paintings of her were prominently placed. It would have been nice if she'd lived to old age. Then I could have had a glimpse of what I'd probably look like when I got old. But, as they say in fairytales, alas, it was not to be. Maybe that was better for my sanity anyway. What if we didn't age gracefully?

I would have loved the castle completely, if its size and opulence hadn't completely overwhelmed me. And it wasn't my responsibility. Okay, sure, that was two huge strikes against it. How was I going to find any secrets about Sid's twin that the Dead Duke may have left? Where did I even start? The Dead Duke must have had an office or a study or something. I just had to find it. And not get lost. Trail of breadcrumbs, anyone?

Gibson let us in through heavy double doors to a sumptuous bedroom, complete with a fireplace and ornate four-poster bed covered in expensive silk bedspreads and pillows. This time, however, the bed was not turned down and covered in rose petals. Guess that was just a wedding night thing. Still, a bit disappointing. Where had the romance gone?

There was a sofa at the foot of the bed. Nightstands on either side. An easy chair nearby and one by the windows. A dressing table. A desk. A small, round table. And matching walk-in closets. Again, it was all from another century. The driver had delivered our bags to the closet. Refreshments, including scones and a teapot covered with a cozy that matched the yellow décor of the room, sat on the table near the windows, along with a beautifully wrapped package in deep blue paper and a fresh bouquet of red roses. Riggins' gaze skimmed it almost too casually.

Gibson gave him a questioning look. "Is everything as you requested, sir?"

Riggins' gaze landed on the package. He raised a brow. "That's from...?"

"Yes, sir. It arrived this morning."

"Perfect. Thank you, Gibson."

"I'll let you get settled. Dinner is at seven in the dining room tonight, as requested."

Riggins nodded. "Yes, very good."

"Text me if you need anything, sir. It's the easiest way." Then Gibson disappeared, closing the door behind him nearly silently.

Riggins didn't say anything more about the package. I figured he'd get to it in due time. Riggins was like that. He liked to build anticipation. He ambled casually to the refreshments, removed the cozy, and poured a cup of tea, glancing sexily at me. "Tea? Scone?"

Anytime he looked at me like that, my heart stopped and I became breathless.

I hoped the feeling never went away. And yet it was unnerving at the same time. And heartbreaking when I considered that our relationship was only business, with maybe a pinch of blossoming friendship thrown in for good measure.

"It *is* teatime," I said. "And I'm hungry. So sure. When in England..."

He poured me a cup. "Sugar? Milk?"

I stuck my tongue out. "Milk? In my tea?" I shivered dramatically to highlight my disgust.

"You're English now, duchess. Remember?"

"Let's not get carried away right off the bat." I smiled demurely and sweetly at him.

"As you wish." He held up a sugar cube in a pair of silver tongs.

"One lump, please."

He dropped it in my tea and handed me the delicate, probably priceless antique china cup, and a silver spoon to stir it. Which I did, and licked the spoon seductively just to tease Riggins. Yes, here I was with a silver spoon literally in my mouth. And my child would be born with one, too, so to speak. If Riggins and I ever had a child.

I blew on my tea and took a sip, letting it swirl around my mouth so I could savor the full body of it. "This tea is heavenly." I was surprised it was so good. "Like nothing I've ever tasted."

"You can't beat English tea. So they say," Riggins said.

I nodded. "Try it. It has a natural honey-like flavor to it." I took another sip, trying to identify the flavor undertones. My baking training kicking in. "I'll have to ask Gibson what kind of tea it is. Or the kitchen staff."

Riggins took a sip and agreed with me.

I selected a scone and looked around the room, with its yellow-gold theme and patterned silk wallpaper. "I hope there's good cell coverage here in the castle, or we'll need an old-fashioned intercom. I mean, if you're wandering around this place and get lost and your cell phone dies, you could be lost for years before anyone finds you." I shuddered for effect.

Riggins grinned and mimicked looking lost and pressing a fake intercom. "I'm in a room with a moose," he said, quoting an old Washington State Lotto commercial.

I cracked up laughing. "I really do feel like I've woken up in a Washington State Lotto commercial. This is too much. All we need now is a zip line down to the nearest coffee shop and we'll be just as upscale. Because we are on a hill so we can look down on our neighbors—"

"I think when this place was built, it was built on hill so that it was easier to defend against marauders with weapons like arrows, tar, and boiling oil," he said.

"I don't think we need boiling oil anymore, except for French fries and donuts." I was having fun and getting carried away as I drank more of my tea. These last few weeks had been a total dream—Riggins, his house on the lake, Wareswood, the wedding, the yacht, the private plane, and now a castle.

"And if I open a door to one of the rooms and find a forest inside, I'm hyperventilating and passing out," I said, referring to several more commercials. "I've had so much over-gorging on wealth the last few days, I think I'm getting wealth hangover."

"That's too bad." He set his teacup down on the table, picked up the wrapped package, and held it out to me. His grin turned lecherous. "This is for you. My wedding gift to you."

"I wasn't expecting a wedding present." To be honest, I'd barely managed to get him a wedding *ring*. I panicked. Had he been expecting a groom's gift from me? That was traditional, wasn't it? Then again, our courtship, engagement, and marriage were anything but.

He started to pull it away. "If you don't want it—"

"Let's not be hasty. I'm probably not over the legal luxury limit *just* yet. And I'm not driving anywhere. I can probably make room for one more excess." I held his gaze and smiled sexily, kittenishly. "Just how extravagant *is* it?"

"Deliciously extravagant. Fantasy-making." His eyes danced and his voice was low and sexy.

"Oh, crap." Now he really had my attention. Fantasy-making? I bit my lip like I was really weighing accepting it. But it was just a formality. I was taking that thing no matter what. "In that case, maybe just *one* more luxurious item before I call it quits for the day."

I set my tea down and took the package from him. It was heavier than I expected, and large. I hefted it, trying to guess what it might be. My first inclination had been jewelry. But the box was too large for a ring, or a bracelet, or even a necklace.

"Open it," he urged.

I bit my lip, concentrating as I pulled the string of the bow and the ribbon fell away. I took my time carefully removing the wrapping, which was clearly store paper, the kind you got in Europe, not the U.S. The paper fell away to reveal a jewelry box, a tall, large jewelry box with the name of one of England's top jewelers embossed in gold on it.

Riggins watched me closely. I hesitated. The hinge of the box was stiff. It took some effort before it sprang open to reveal a brilliant, sparkling diamond tiara sitting on a rich velvet bed.

"*Oh.*" I took a deep breath to keep from crying.

"Duchesses are expected to wear a tiara to special events. There's evidently a collection of them that have been passed down from past duchesses in the safe. But I thought you needed your own." He sounded almost nervous.

Which was so touching and endearing that I almost believed he loved me. I stared at him with tears sparkling in my eyes.

"Don't you like it? I took the liberty of designing it. We can have it reworked—"

"I'm speechless." I wiped my eyes with the back of my hand. "It's the most beautiful thing ever." I threw myself into his arms and wrapped them around his neck, still holding the box. "Thank you." I kissed him until it became obvious that we already had a room, so maybe we should use it.

He pried me away and took the jewelry box from me. "Let me put this on you." He whispered in my ear as he removed the tiara from the box, "I want to see you in this and nothing else."

"Why, duke! The things you say. That's not very duchesslike behavior you're suggesting. Is this a special occasion?" I was wearing jeans, not an evening gown.

"It is when the duke's around. And yes, it's a very special occasion." He nuzzled my neck, pressing hot kisses into it. "The first time we're going to do the deed in our castle, duchess." He had a wicked gleam in his eye as he pulled away and set the tiara on my head.

"We're supposed to be resting," I said playfully, as I unbuttoned his shirt.

"We'll have plenty of time to rest. *After.*"

CHAPTER SIX

R *iggins*
We dressed for dinner that evening. Haley in an evening gown my Flash merch buyers had helped her pick out. Me in a white tux. Like we were from a bygone era. Maybe the early 1900s. Haley wore her tiara. Which pleased me and drove me mad with lust. I kept picturing her naked with those diamonds glistening against her silver hair as I made love to her.

She was the most beautiful, enticing woman I'd ever known. And becoming more so every day. She made me laugh. Even at dinner. As we sat in the formal dining room at the end of a table that could easily seat dozens,

Haley whispered that she felt like we were playing dress-up. It was a little-girl fantasy come to life. Everything I gave her and every new experience delighted her. I wanted her to be happy. Wanted it so damn much. But she had no sense of entitlement. Made no demands for romance. I knew what would thrill her most. Now that the Dead Duke had gotten his wish and drawn me to the castle, I was going to find Sid's cure. And then? I was growing less sure I wanted out of this arranged marriage. But not convinced. Where Haley saw sentiment, history, and a family, all I could see as I looked around the castle was work and commitment.

Haley was already more part of this place than I was. Or maybe could ever hope to be. Maybe that was appropriate. I would have given it to her, if that had been possible.

The dining room was green. Deep green. Not my favorite shade of the color. Filled with antiques and filigree. With more of those damned paintings of ancestors staring down at us. Approvingly or disapprovingly, it was hard to tell. All I could say was that some of them looked exceedingly arrogant. And many of them had what women always described as my sexy smirk.

Was smirking sexy? Hell, I had no idea. I did it unconsciously. But women thought it indicated confidence. And confidence was sexy. The smirk every few generations, and sometimes something about the eyes, where the only links I could find between the men in the paintings, my predecessors, and myself.

I didn't like the arrogant ones. Others looked silly in their stiff white ruffs and frills. I still hadn't seen a portrait of the Dead Duke. I wasn't sure I wanted to. If he had the smirk... Shit.

There was probably a gigantic painting of him in the entry, hanging in the place of honor. I ignored it when we came in, fearing I'd give in to my anger and fantasies of slashing it with a knife. But there was no reason to destroy a valuable piece of art.

This whole place looked more and more like an albatross to me the more I saw of it. Beautiful, yes. But lethal to the lifestyle I'd carved out for myself.

Annoyed, I became nitpicky. The Wi-Fi signal was weak. Being connected to the outside world was essential to me. How was I supposed to work without Wi-Fi? Apparently it hadn't been as important to the reclusive Dead Duke. First thing I was going to update to high-speed Internet. If that were possible out here in the sticks. It was a small annoyance, but indicative of dozens of others that were sure to pop up.

The next morning, Tuesday, I got up early for my meeting with Bird, the groundskeeper. Aptly named, at least. At his request, I met him at a stand of trees on the edge of one of my meadows. Gibson gave me directions. It was embarrassing to have to get directions to find my way on my own property.

I found Bird dressed in archaic-looking tweeds, including hat, in colors that blended fairly well with the surroundings. An old-fashioned version of camouflage. He sat on the ground with his back against a tree with a high-powered rifle at his side, and a pair of binoculars held to his eyes as he watched a herd of deer in the meadow.

I wasn't a hunter, but I knew enough to approach quietly. I was dressed in jeans, boots, and hunting jacket at Gibson's suggestion. Earlier, I'd ordered it, also on Gibson's recommendation, and had it sent to the castle before our arrival. Caring about the game was part of my job.

Bird looked up and nodded slowly as I approached and took a seat next to him. We watched the deer together in silence for what seemed like forever. They were fine animals. Healthy and strong. Bird was doing a good job with them as far as I could tell.

Finally he whispered to me, "Fancy venison for dinner tonight, Your Grace?"

I grimaced.

Bird nodded. "Beautiful animals; you're right. We don't generally hunt them. But from time to time we need to cull the herd. Otherwise they overpopulate and the vegetation can't support them."

I nodded. He made sense. But it seemed a shame.

"Does usually outnumber bucks by as much as ten to one. Right now, many of the does are pregnant." He pointed with the tip of his rifle. "We try to cull the herd early in the fall season. But I shoot does year round when I have to. That one." He nodded. "She isn't pregnant. Probably miscarried earlier. We'll take her."

I nodded again.

He crouched and put the deer in his sights. I held my breath. He pulled the trigger. The animal fell to the ground. The rest of the deer scattered.

"Nice shot," I said. I was a city boy. I didn't particularly like seeing my dinner killed. It was much more impersonal to buy meat already butchered at the market. Better yet, to get a fully cooked meal at a restaurant.

"The game supports the estate. We put meat on His Grace's table year round. Venison, pheasant, quail, even fish of various kinds." Bird gave me a look, challenging me to disagree.

I nodded again. Why should I make changes? The game could feed the staff in my absence. My long planned absences.

He relaxed somewhat and stood. I stood with him. When he faced me full-on, he reminded me of someone. But I couldn't think whom. We all get that feeling from time to time. He probably reminded me of some character actor on TV.

"Bird, sir," he said, introducing himself.

"I guess you call me duke." I wasn't certain.

He grinned. "Yes, sir."

"Have you been the gamekeeper here long?" I hadn't had time to study all the staff history and résumés.

"Since I was a young man. Like my father before me and his before him. There have been Birds taking care of the wildlife here as long as there have been Feldhems ruling.

"My family history here goes back almost seven hundred years. Since before there were surnames. Where do you think we got the name Bird? My ancestor was John of the birds, in charge of the fowl on the land. Then it just became family name of Bird.

"Those of us who weren't gamekeepers mostly worked on the estate in some way. One of my great, great, however many great-grandfathers helped build the grand staircase in the great hall. No, we Birds are tied to the land." He eyed me cautiously. "I hope you'll come to love it like we do. The old duke, he sure did for certain. Loved that old man. He was always good to my family. We miss him.

"Now me, I have my son, who'll be coming to work beside me when he graduates university. He's studying biology and wildlife management, same as I did. Compliments of the late duke, who insisted on paying all of his expenses. Claimed it was an investment in the future of the estate, nothing more. His way of covering his kindness." Bird beamed with pride. "You'll have no worries about the game being properly managed."

"Excellent." I smiled and nodded toward the pasture, not certain the Dead Duke was covering anything. "What do we do now? About the doe?"

"It has to be gutted and hung to drain and cure. I have the truck just there." He pointed to the road. "I'll haul the doe back to the castle to clean and hang." He gave me a pointed look, like he was testing me.

"I'll give you a hand." I wasn't exactly eager.

He smiled. "That's good of you, sir."

I was suddenly grateful for Gibson's wardrobe suggestion. "You liked the late duke?" I said, dubious. His description didn't match the cunning, conniving old bastard I didn't know or love.

"Oh, he was a good one. My grandfather was his gamekeeper when the old duke was a young man. My grandfather couldn't praise him enough. He turned the estate around. Saved it, he did. The old duke's father was a gambler and a big spender. Had no regard or sense of responsibility for the people who should have been like family to him.

"My grandfather said of course it was tragic the way he died on the *Titanic*. The duchess, too. Though she wasn't so much better. But his early death saved Witham House. The trustee who managed it for the baby duke was a good man. He did his best and saw to it the young duke had a proper upbringing.

"The late duke was one of a kind. Like a grandfather to me and mine. No, I don't have a bad word to say about the old duke. Not one. He was the best of men. Without him, my family wouldn't still be here, where we belong."

Haley
Riggins left early to meet with Mr. Bird, the gamekeeper. Leaving me to sleep a little later and fend for myself. Very embarrassingly, I had to text Gibson to ask where the kitchen was, and what about breakfast? Crazy that in my own temporary home, I felt shy about going to the kitchen and grabbing a bite to eat. And, truthfully, had no idea where it was. I assumed it was fully stocked, at least if dinner last night was any indication.

Instead of directing me to the kitchen, Gibson brought up a breakfast tray. "Oh, it's no trouble, ma'am," he said to me. "I'm used to it. I brought the old duke all of his meals on trays for years. He was very sharp to the end. But not so steady on his feet." He shook his head sadly. "His body gave out well before his mind."

I sensed a deep affection for the Dead Duke. Which was completely surprising to me.

After breakfast, Gibson gave me a tour of the house. Which, I had to say, was at least as good as, and probably better, than Beth's tour of Wareswood. And, of course, Witham House outshone Wareswood in every way.

Gibson was exceptionally knowledgeable about everything from architecture to furniture and artwork. He could have been a historian. He was also witty and funny. I liked him. But although he was pleasant and respectful, I sensed he was wary of me. I hadn't yet proved myself. As far as he knew, I could turn out to be the most evil of duchesses.

And I was American, an interloper in his land. It was quite possible he'd been hoping Lady Rose would be the new duchess. I had to earn his confidence.

He showed me the kitchen first, so I could thank the cook. I was usually very light on breakfast—a bowl of cold cereal, a cup of coffee. A pastry if I was feeling indulgent and decadent. Many mornings when I worked at the bakery I skipped breakfast and just grabbed something on my morning break. Most times, one of our mishaps.

Our head cook was actually a chef, a five-star chef who preferred the quiet life on the estate to fame in the city. We must have paid well. He'd worked for the Dead

Duke for many years, preparing a diet heavy on restrictions. He'd introduced himself last night at dinner. He seemed pleased to be working for younger people who could eat anything. We had a pleasant discussion about it. He didn't come in until the afternoon to prepare dinner. Occasionally he came in to make lunch. He had several assistants who prepared breakfast and lunch. One for weekdays and one on the weekends, and a few extras as needed, or if one of the regulars was out sick or on vacation. Alice, the weekday breakfast cook, was in. I introduced myself.

"My! If you don't look like the late duke's first duchess, Helen. At least like her likeness."

I laughed. "I've heard that before. I love the tea I had yesterday when we arrived and again this morning," I said, trying to make conversation. "I'm usually a coffee girl. I'm from Seattle. What else could I be? We're known for our coffee addiction. But I think I'm already becoming addicted to the tea. What kind is it?"

Alice was a plump, friendly woman in her late fifties, I guessed. "Oh, that!" She looked pleased. "That's the late duke's special blend. We call it Duke Witham. Like Earl Grey, only better. Though not a classic. Yet. It's a recipe that's been in the family for years.

"I'm glad you like it. Shows you're one of us. I'll write down that it's a favorite of yours and make sure you get it as often as you like."

I liked Alice, too. But once again, I sensed some reserve in her. She was withholding her judgment, maybe, and her confidence and loyalty, until she knew me better. She showed me around the kitchen. Finally, I timidly asked about getting myself a snack. And my own breakfast sometimes.

"Raid the larder anytime, ma'am, surely!" She nodded. "Just let me know if you use the last of anything so I can reorder."

That was a relief. *Wait!* Wasn't I mistress of this place, not her?

"The kitchen is lovely. I'd like to be able to come in and bake sometimes, too. I love baking. I went to pastry school and worked in a bakery until very recently." Maybe I shouldn't have admitted that. But didn't everyone know? It had been all over the news.

"Anytime, ma'am." Alice seemed genuine.

After chatting with Alice in our reasonably cozy kitchen for a while longer—cozy only because I was comfortable in large commercial kitchens—Gibson continued our tour.

"Are there any pictures of Helen, the late duchess?" I asked Gibson. "And the dead, I mean, late duke. Maybe as a young man? Or, at least, a younger man. If so, I'd like to see them. I'm dying of curiosity about the late duke."

"Oh, there are pictures of *all* of his duchesses, ma'am. Remember, there were three. But I daresay Helen was his favorite. His one true love. It's rather obvious when you see the portrait gallery. And yes, there are portraits, *and* photographs.

"I think you'll find the late duke was a spectacular man in his prime. Tall and handsome. With movie-star-like charisma. He had it right up to the end. That air of command. Presence, I might say.

"But kind and compassionate. Always looking after his own. And his own extended to the staff and the people of the village. No, the late duke was a man to be emulated."

Gibson glanced at me with a questioning look. "We're hoping the new duke will live up to his predecessor's reputation, if I may say so." He looked almost embarrassed. As if he'd overstepped. "My apologies, ma'am. You seem so familiar, as if we've known you for years, that I forgot myself and spoke out of turn."

I was pleased I seemed familiar. I wanted the staff to feel comfortable with me.

"No. You're fine." I smiled at him. "The new duke is tall and handsome," I said with a smile. "*I* think so, at least. Since I didn't know the late duke, I have no idea how he compares otherwise. But Riggins treats his employees very well, from what I know. Everyone wants to work at Flashionista. It has a great reputation for being employee-friendly and having generous benefits. Riggins is an astute businessman. Like the late duke."

Gibson nodded. "The duke's portrait is in the upper guard chamber. I'm surprised you didn't notice it when you came in, ma'am. We walked past it on the way to the bedroom corridor."

"Mmmmm," I said, trying to remember. "I may have. But I wouldn't have known it was him. I was so overwhelmed with everything, I was looking but not seeing." I laughed.

"Yes, of course. How would you?" Gibson said, leading the way. "The portraits of the duchesses are in the gallery hall, along with another portrait of the duke from later in life. A portrait of the first duchess and the late duke together hangs in the great hall in a position of honor. His personal favorite photograph of the duchess and him hangs in his study. But, as you requested, first we'll meet the young duke."

"Great! I'd like that. I'm totally curious about him." I paused. "I wish I could have known him."

"You would have loved him, I'm sure. As we all did. This way." Gibson led me to the upper guard chamber.

A reception room, it was as magnificent as the staircase and all done in matching white Carrara marble, like the staircase as well. It was also done in the Italian Renaissance style with a stucco ceiling and terrazzo floor. Marble statues stood at the far wall. The artwork was all family portraits, some of them done by famous masters. The frieze paintings depicted famous battles from the district's history.

Now that I wasn't tired and was looking for it, the Dead Duke's portrait was obvious. Gibson had been polite to agree that I wouldn't have known it was the Dead Duke. That was obviously laughable. He was the only duke dressed in the much more modern fashion of the 1930s. Dark suit with strong shoulders, two buttons buttoned. Vest. Diagonal striped tie. Starched white shirt, just the collar and one cuff showing. High-waisted, pleated slacks, one hand tucked dashingly in his pocket, pushing back part of the suit coat in an "I'm so sexy" pose. White kerchief in his pocket. The other arm rested on a decorative pedestal. His hand was casual and relaxed. He wore a signet ring with the ducal seal prominently on his pinkie.

He was looking down and to the side, the whites of his eyes stark and visible. Though he wasn't looking out at the viewer, his eyes were arresting. His lush, dark hair was parted on the side, slicked back over itself on top—slicked back on the side, too. He had a thin, closely cropped, elegant moustache. Very Clark Gable-esque. And equally handsome.

He was stunning. Best yet, one corner of his mouth was turned up in a fun-loving, audaciously sexy smirk. He looked like he was toying with the world and the world really was his oyster. Oh. My. Goodness. He was hot. Classic movie star gorgeous.

"That's the Dead Duke?" I forgot myself as I stared at him, trying not to let my jaw drop.

Gibson grinned. "Quite the ladies' man, wasn't he? You can see how Helen must have felt when she first saw him. He had the charm to match, ma'am. Right up to the end."

I shook my head and grinned at Gibson. "After seeing this, I hate to imagine him old and crippled."

Gibson nodded. "Old age does us all in."

"You should have set me straight earlier. I must have been really tired to miss this picture. And there's no way I shouldn't have been able to tell it was him just from his style of dress.

"Tell me about him, Gibson. I want to know everything. Let's start with his favorite room. Will you show me that?" I was eager to gain Gibson's confidence. As the Dead Duke's butler, it was likely he knew something about the late duke's business. Maybe he knew something about Sid's twin. But I had to proceed cautiously.

"Oh, he loved the library. And his study, of course. I'll show you both. After the gallery and the great hall, ma'am. We don't want to forget about the duchesses."

The gallery was a long hallway hung with portrait paintings through the ages. One side of the hall was windows. Gibson explained about the special glass of the windows that protected the paintings from aging prematurely and lit them to full advantage. And the security in place at the castle to prevent break-ins and burglaries. Riggins, I took it, had hired extra security to keep the paparazzi away as well. I had been insulated from it, but I was sure a media storm was raging about our wedding. With the light streaming in, the gallery was absolutely stunning. Really, I was running out of adjectives to describe the rooms of the castle.

Gibson led me to the far end of the gallery and stopped in front of a trio of portraits of women. One was clearly from the 1970s. She was a classic beauty of a woman. And clearly much younger than the Dead Duke. One from the 1950s, also a striking woman. He had good taste. But a man of his looks, power, status, title, and charm could have anyone he wanted, couldn't he?

The last one was from the 1930s. You could tell the era just by the fashions the women wore.

"That's the third duchess," Gibson said. "That's the second." He paused and looked at me. "And that one is Helen. I'm sure I don't need to tell you that. Viewing it must be like looking in a mirror. You look just like her.

"I never knew her, obviously, but, if you don't mind me saying so, you look so much like her picture you gave us all rather a shock. Of course, we'd seen your pictures in the tabloids and everywhere. But in person, the resemblance is even more striking. It's clear you're her great-niece."

I nodded. "Yes, I am."

In my possibly biased opinion, Helen was the least beautiful of the duchesses. Even my bias couldn't overcome the truth. People must have wondered what he'd seen in her, and whispered that, looks-wise, they were mismatched. He had to have married her just for her money. What do you call the male version of a gold digger? An opportunist?

Despite this, if you saw the paintings, you were caught by Helen's magnetism. It was potent; it jumped off the canvas.

"It's obvious now why the duke was partial to you and wanted you to be mistress of his dukedom. He was a sentimental, romantic man."

I studied the portrait of Helen. It was a better picture than the one at Wareswood. Since I looked so obviously like her, it would be vain of me to say she was beautiful. Clearly, I wasn't beautiful. But, again, she had a presence that was obvious in the picture, just like the Dead Duke did. Charisma and personality can make up for a large deficit in the looks department. I could see how they could make a striking couple.

"It's a nice painting," I said, deliberately understating my opinion of it.

"Oh, yes. Valuable, too. Done by one of the famous painters of the day. Not as valuable as the van Dycks, or some of the others, obviously. Might be one day. She was a beautiful woman."

His pronouncement startled me. If he was trying to get on my good side, I wasn't easily flattered.

"Think so?" I squinted, trying to see it. "Not beautiful, I don't think. Not like the other duchesses. But there's something about her. She has a spark. You can see it in the look in her eyes."

"I beg to differ, ma'am. In my opinion, she far outshines the later duchesses. We'll have to agree to disagree. Would you like to see the great hall?"

The great hall was a great, cavernous, arched room that stood on the site of the original great hall and felt like a cathedral to me.

"It's easy to imagine one of the medieval dukes meting out justice here," I said, looking around, glad that I wasn't at the mercy of an unforgiving feudal lord.

Gibson nodded. "I would agree. These days, we only use it for receptions and charity events, of course. This way." He led me directly to the portrait of the Dead Duke and duchess.

What Gibson had said earlier was immediately clear. The painting was almost scandalous in its sensuality. Although they were fully clothed and sedately posed, the way the Dead Duke looked at Helen—well, it was something out of a great romance.

His fingers possessively clutched her waist, bunching the fabric of her dress. His eyes sparkled, evocative of lust and desire. Full of love and heat, and directed in their full intensity at Helen. There was that smirk, that quirk of one corner of his sensuous, full lips, again. He was just as handsome, if not more so, than he was in the painting in the upper guard's chamber.

Viewing it, I felt like I'd walked in on a private moment and should quietly back out.

"*Oh.*" I swallowed hard and turned to Gibson, who was also staring at it in wonder. "I see what you mean. I take it there are no pictures of him looking at the other duchesses like that?"

CHAPTER SEVEN

*H*aley
"There's a photograph of the late duke and duchess together in the late duke's private study. If you like this painting, you'll love it," Gibson said. "First, though, perhaps the library?"

If Riggins ever looked at me like that, I would faint dead away from happiness. It was every woman's goal to have a man she loved look at her like he wanted to possess her. Want her that much. Adore her more than anything. To gaze at her like she was his life's blood. As much as I wanted to get my hands on the Dead Duke's study, I had to pry myself away from the painting.

Gibson and I chatted pleasantly on the walk to the library.

"You and the late duke were close?" I asked, with an ulterior motive, hoping he knew something about Sid's possible twin.

"I worked for him for several decades. I knew his tastes and likes, and his personal opinion on many matters, yes. I admired him. And he was a good employer. But close, as in a friend, no, I don't think so, ma'am."

I nodded, fighting my desire to ask him more, like if the Dead Duke had ever confided anything about business to him. But that seemed like going too far too soon.

"The library was the duke's favorite room," Gibson said as we approached it. "He was a learned man. An introvert, you might say. A gregarious introvert, but fueled by time alone to think and recharge. Too many social engagements drained him.

"As he aged, he gave them up entirely. Though if you ask me, it wasn't just the desire to recharge alone. He said he'd lived too long. He was bored and his body had failed him. I don't think the duke was necessarily a vain man. But his looks had faded, too. He'd been used to being admired by the ladies, you see. And being strong and virile. I believe he preferred to be remembered that way, as opposed to the shrunken shell of a man he'd become at the end."

"I don't really blame him," I said, sympathetic. I wasn't looking forward to becoming a frail little old lady either. "I imagine losing your looks is something of a comedown. Even though the alternative isn't a happy thought either."

Gibson smiled. "No, indeed. But a long life has its downsides, too. And the late duke felt them keenly. He lived through a great many struggles and personal tragedies. Planning for the estate's future kept him going, I believe. For the last many years, it was the *only* thing he lived for."

Gibson made me almost feel sorry for the Dead Duke.

"He loved to read and study," Gibson continued. "A very intelligent man from the beginning. With a high IQ. Around 160." Gibson's chest puffed with pride, as if his status was somehow elevated by working for such a smart man. "Genius level, they say. Always got top marks at school."

An evil genius to some, I thought. I'd seen firsthand how diabolically clever he was. But 160? How did I compete against that?

As Gibson threw open the doors to the library, my pulse raced. My heart plunged into my stomach as I stepped in. *Crap.* The place was as large as the Seattle Public Library, if not larger. How would I find his secrets in a place like this?

I gulped. "Impressive."

"It is, isn't it?" Gibson looked around with the same sense of awe I had. Which spoke to how extraordinary it was, that he was still impressed after having been around it for decades.

Bookshelves stuffed with books reached to the incredibly high ceiling that was at least two stories tall. So high that rolling ladders went along the cases to allow you to climb to the top shelf to snag a book. Nearly all the books were leather bound and works of art. Gibson went on about how many valuable first editions there were in the collection. The family histories on the shelves. Something about an original copy of the King James Bible, and other treasures. And the challenges of providing archival conditions to preserve the books. The most valuable volumes were evidently housed in a special, climate-controlled room. Riggins wasn't going to like hearing that. Running a valuable library on top of everything else?

Without prompting, Gibson pointed out the Dead Duke's favorite spot to sit and read. And named a few of his favorite books, including a volume titled *Lady Witham's Great Game*. Which seemed an incongruous book for him to like. I made a mental note to check it, and the others, out.

"How are the books shelved?" I asked out of curiosity. And so I knew how to search them. "The usual way—the Dewey Decimal System?" I was only half joking. Using the Dewey Decimal system would have required labeling and categorizing all the books, including volumes that had been on the shelves for hundreds of years.

"Shelving the books in a logical manner has always been a challenge," Gibson said. "This library was in existence well before the Dewey Decimal System was invented. Many of the titles are shelved alphabetically by author and then by title. There are a few shelves that house the late duke's personal favorites.

"And, of course, there are scrolls as well." He pointed to drawers and cupboards. "The late duke had everything entered into an electronic database. It was quite the job. It's searchable by author, title, and subject matter. It also gives the shelf the book should be on. The local librarian in the village was most helpful and has a good grasp on the intricacies of this library."

"Yay for modern electronics." I looked around the room again. It seemed to go on forever. I couldn't overstate the size of it if I tried.

It smelled like old leather, yellowing pages, dust, and a hint of cigar smoke lingering from ages past. In short, it smelled like antiquity. Which Riggins hated. I didn't think all the room fresheners in the world would mask it. Nor should they. Not if it were up to me, anyway. It smelled exactly like a library should.

"I'd like access to the database. Like the late duke, I love to read. I'm also fascinated by history. Particularly if there's any history of the castle and the family..."

Gibson nodded. "I'll make sure you get it."

We moved on to the Dead Duke's private study.

Gibson unlocked a door and let me in. "This was His Grace's inner sanctum." He sighed heavily, sadly. "I can almost still see him sitting at his desk just there."

My heart raced with excitement at the sight of it. This room was cozy and personal. Filled with the Dead Duke's personality. His intimate objects. The books he loved best. His favorite art. His favorite chair. Books lining the shelves. File drawers my fingers itched to search. Where would he have hidden information about

Sid's possible twin? Was it here at all? Or sealed and locked in a vault in Mr. Thorne's law firm? I paused to compose my thoughts and process my first impressions. I could almost feel the Dead Duke's presence in the room. Not necessarily in a paranormal way. My sense of smell was highly sensitive. I inhaled deeply. It was just possible I detected a hint of what must have been his cologne lingering in the air. And lemon polish and dusting clothes.

As crazy as it sounded, I liked what I saw. The room indicated a sense of humor that was comforting. And at odds with the opinion I had of a stern and humorless man.

I decided the Dead Duke must have been meticulous about his personal toiletry and cleanliness. There wasn't a hint of that old-people smell at all.

Gibson was spot on. The room looked eerily as if the Dead Duke had just stepped out to grab a cup of tea. His glasses sat by a landline phone. There was a pen next to a notebook, as if he'd been about to jot himself a note.

The room had clearly been dusted and cleaned. Every surface gleamed.

"Has anyone touched this room since the duke's death?" I asked.

"The cleaning staff has been in regularly, like always." Gibson sounded almost insulted that I would have thought otherwise.

I pressed on anyway. "Has it been picked up and tidied?" I looked around. The room was fairly neat, but not pristine like most of the other rooms. It was lived it. Which gave it that feeling that he was still alive and using it.

"No. It's as he left it. The duke gave specific instructions that nothing was to be moved from its original location until instructed by the new duke." Gibson lifted his chin, obviously defensive. "He was adamant about that. We respected his wishes. As eccentric as he seemed at times, the late duke had a reason for everything he did. Though it wasn't always obvious at first."

I nodded. *Strange.* I would love to poke around on my own. I made a mental note to tell Riggins about it and get his opinion.

"Wonderful." I had to smooth ruffled feathers. "I'm so glad you did. I'm sure the late duke wanted us to know something about who he was as a person. And I'm glad to get the chance."

Gibson relaxed and nodded, at least slightly appeased. "This is the portrait I brought you here to see."

Hanging on the wall opposite the Dead Duke's desk, in direct line of sight, where he could stare at it as he worked, was a photograph of the Dead Duke and Helen in an embrace that belonged on the cover of a romance novel. Or in the bedroom. Once again, it was breathtaking for its passion. Classic and classy. Obviously taken by a skilled photographer who'd captured their kiss to perfection.

"I feel like I should be blushing," I said, my gaze fixed on it. "It's like a beautiful accident. I feel like I'm intruding on a private moment, but I can't look away." I took a step closer.

Gibson laughed and nodded. "Yes, ma'am. I think we all feel that way. You see what I mean now?"

He walked over to stand in front of the black-and-white photo with its sharp and contrasting lighting done at the hands of a skilled portrait photographer, and not yellowed or faded by time. Thank goodness they didn't have color photography back them. This picture would have been sepia by now. It was matted and expensively framed to match the style of the room.

"It's hung exactly there ever since I've been here, and that's decades. I heard directly from staff members that were with the late duke when it was originally taken that it's been on that wall since he received it from the photographer.

"After she died, he wouldn't let anyone touch that picture for years. Not even to dust it. He dusted it himself.

"He left her bedroom exactly as it was when she died, too. Locked it up. Wouldn't let anyone in there for a good decade. Not even to clean. Gave the second duchess a different room, even though it was less conveniently located and not the mistress' suite. Until she finally talked the duke into reopening Helen's room."

Gibson paused, acting like he'd said too much. "I don't want to give the wrong impression. The duke loved *all* his wives. He valued the second duchess' opinions, obviously. But Helen was special."

Gibson studied the photo. His voice became soft with emotion. "The duke never got over her. *Never.* That's what everyone said. Even though I never knew her and never saw them together in person, the truth of it was clear to me from more than just the stories."

I frowned, puzzled by this foreign picture of the Dead Duke, so different from my own thoughts on him. It didn't seem kind to me to keep this photo up when he was married to someone else. Especially in a place where he saw it every working hour here. Why did he do it? If what Gibson said was true, it must have killed the Dead Duke to look at his young, vibrant first wife day after day and not be able to have her or talk to her. On one level, it seemed like a cruel kind of self-torture.

"Didn't the other duchesses object?" I asked. "They weren't jealous?"

Gibson shook his head. "If they did, he didn't listen. This was his private space and absolute domain. No one told him what to do here. Rumors were the duchesses weren't allowed in here ever. It's possible they didn't know."

"His man cave?" I said.

"Yes, I guess you might call it that."

"I hope the duchesses had their private domains, too." Fair was fair.

Gibson studied the picture with me. "There are no pictures like this of him with the other duchesses, you understand."

I inhaled deeply. "I do. I definitely *do*."

We stared at it in companionable silence. "Helen's bedroom—is it still the same?"

"Oh, no, ma'am. The second duchess never used it herself. But she had it completely redone, in as much as she could while still maintaining the décor of the castle and historic value.

"The third duchess used Helen's room as her own and put her own touches on it again."

I nodded, disappointed. "The study was locked when we arrived. May I have a key? I'd like to come here and look at it whenever I want. Get to know the late duke for myself." And look for clues to Sid's cure.

"You'll have to get the current duke's permission before I can give you a key, ma'am. This is his private space now."

Riggins

After a day looking over the estate and the books, I wanted to unwind and make love to my duchess. Damn, thoughts of her intruded at the least convenient times.

When I finally got her in the bedroom, she playfully pushed me fully dressed onto my back on the open bed and climbed on top of me, straddling me and rubbing up against me, laughing playfully. She was barefoot and wearing jeans and a pullover sweater.

"Finally, I got you alone! We can talk, *really* talk. Though the walls might have ears for all we know." She laughed again and leaned over to kiss me lightly as her long, lavender-tipped silver hair fell over my face.

Her kiss was just a tease, nothing more. She knew full well what she was doing as she rubbed her crotch against mine and braced her hands against my chest. She sat up and unbuttoned my shirt. "So? Tell me about your day and I'll tell you about mine."

"Haven't we been over this at dinner?" My shirt fell open. "I helped gut a deer. We'll be having venison for dinner soon."

She traced a line down my stomach with the tip of her fingernail until I shuddered pleasantly beneath her touch, aching with want and holding back.

She smiled seductively. "Learned something new or knew how to do it?"

"Learned something new."

"Well, there's that." She bent and ran her tongue around my nipple.

"We could have said all this in front of the staff." My breath caught as she started to suck. "Your day?"

"I toured the house. Including the Dead Duke's study. I saw some beautiful pictures of him." Her words were hot against my chest. "The young Dead Duke was surprisingly hot."

She sat up suddenly and pulled her sweater off over her head, tossing it away and unfastening her bra. She tossed that away, too. I never tired of looking at her breasts.

"Do you have a crush on the Dead Duke?" I teased. The thought was impossible. "Is that what has you turned on?"

She grinned and stroked my cheek. "You know, you have his smirk." She leaned forward and kissed the side of my mouth.

"What?" I had the family smirk. I hadn't realized the Dead Duke had it, too. I wasn't sure I should be flattered. "Is that an insult?" I said playfully.

"I love a man with a confident smirk. It's sexy. You turn me on, duke. *You.*"

I reached for her breasts. "I heard a lot about him today myself. Bird painted a completely different picture of him than I have. A flattering picture. Can you believe it?"

"Mmmmmm. Gibson did, too. Seems he was much loved and extremely generous." She unzipped my jeans and peeled them back. "Quite the paradox, isn't he?"

Her breasts budded.

I took her nipple in my hand. "Do you always talk this much during sex?"

She grinned. "You tell me. You're my only." She leaned forward. "I need a favor." Her voice was silky as she reached into my jeans and stroked my dick.

"Are you using sex to get what you want?"

"I am." She kissed me again. Deeply.

I wanted her so badly. "At least you're honest."

She grinned. "I want a key to the Dead Duke's study. I asked Gibson for one. He said the study's yours now and I have to ask you. Apparently I need your permission."

I unzipped her jeans and put my hands around her waist, trying to keep my voice even. "Why do you want it?"

"I want to go through his papers and things. The key to Sid's cure could be there." Her breath caught as I ground against her. "He has to have kept a record of his plans somewhere." Her gaze held mine.

"Show me the office tomorrow. We'll go through it together."

"My key?"

"You have my dick in your hand," I said as smoothly as I could. "This is no way to do business. Do I have any choice?"

"It could be someplace *much* nicer. Warm and moist—"

"Damn. Is it wrong to want you so much?" I slid her jeans down her hips. "I'll give you your key. Now get out of those jeans."

Haley
I took Riggins on a Dead Duke tour, showing him all the portraits, lingering in front of the one in the guard chamber. "You see? He was hot. *Very* hot. I think I'll ask Gibson to move this painting into our bedroom so I can fan-girl over it all the time. He can watch us approvingly as we procreate."

I lowered my voice and whispered into Riggins' ear, "Let him think we're trying to make a baby. Birth control. Our revenge!"

Riggins rolled his eyes. "Over my dead body."

Riggins had procured a key to the Dead Duke's study. The photo of the Dead Duke and duchess in there interested him more.

I took his arm as he studied it. "Told you! You can't look away, can you? The passion just jumps off the photo paper. They clearly love each other—"

Riggins pulled me into his arms and kissed me, mimicking the pose exactly. One arm around my waist. One holding the back of my head. Tongue in my mouth, dancing with mine, seducing me. When he released me, I was breathless.

"So?" I said. "I take it you like this picture."

"The duchess is hot." He raised his eyebrows lecherously.

I laughed. "Glad you think so. Maybe I should start dressing in 1930s fashion."

"Don't you dare! It's pure modern-day Flashionista for you. Now that you're duchess, it's your responsibility to promote the brand."

"Hey, this is our honeymoon. No business." I kissed him lightly.

We broke apart and walked around the office together.

He was obviously curious. "It feels like he should be coming back any minute."

"I know, right? That's exactly what I felt this first time, and still do." I told him what Gibson had told me about nothing being moved on the Dead Duke's orders. "What does he want us to find? What does he want us to know?"

I hoped it was about Sid. But I couldn't tell Riggins that. I'd promised to keep it a secret.

Riggins picked up an art deco paperweight and sat it back down again. "You think he wants us to find something out?"

"I think he wanted us to know him, at the very least. Can't you almost feel him here? His personality shines through. He was a romantic and had a sense of humor. Gibson says he had an IQ of 160."

Riggins raised an eyebrow. "Damn. We knew he was smart."

"I know!" I nodded. "He knew what he was doing to us and forcing us into. That we could easily hate him. "I used to think he didn't care about our opinion of him. That he was some toughened old bastard who didn't give a damn what we, or *anyone*, thought of him. The only legacy he cared about was the dukedom and his public reputation. Now I'm not so sure."

I hesitated, not wanting to sound silly. "I think he wants us to like him. And this is his attempt. He wants us to read his private papers. Find his journals. See how well he ran the estate. How much he loved his duchesses. Get how loyal he was. Feel for him for the tragedies he endured. And respect and love him for all of it."

I extended my arm, indicating the room. "The man who occupied this study isn't the Dead Duke we know. Nor is he the infallible man the staff talks about with so much respect and fondness. Are they wrong? Or are we?"

Riggins turned to me. "We all present different faces to different people. The face he gave us wasn't his most flattering." He took a deep breath. "Are you falling for this?" He indicated the room.

"I don't think this is faked or staged." I almost held back my opinion. "I'm willing to be open-minded and accept, like most of us, he had many facets. That he wasn't either all good or all bad. He was, however, exceptionally goal oriented. He wanted what he wanted and spared nothing to get it. We can agree on that."

Riggins' expression had been hard. It softened as he pulled me close. "Damn. I had no idea I married a woman who looked for the best in everyone."

"Would that have been a deal breaker?"

"Not if I would have known how hot the sex between us would be."

"One-track mind."

"One-track mind? It's our honeymoon. If I don't have sex on the brain now, we're in trouble."

I laughed and pulled away from him. I plopped into the Dead Duke's desk chair, spinning around, surveying his dukedom through the window, and looking over his office. "I like this room."

"Good thing. We're going to be spending a lot of time here in the next weeks." He came up behind me and massaged my neck. "You know he's still manipulating us?"

I nodded, suddenly willing to let him. If he was the man of my first impressions, then we were in trouble. But if he'd been the man the staff knew...

Riggins bent down and lifted the hair off my neck, kissing me near my ear. "Where do we begin, duchess?"

CHAPTER EIGHT

*H*aley
And so our search began for Sid's cure and the things that could bring this wonderful dream marriage to an end. I was working at cross-purposes. I didn't want to lose Riggins. Ever. And he...

He was passionate. And romantic. He made love to me everywhere. Sometimes he joked that he wanted to make love to me in every room in the castle.

I'd laughed. "There are over two hundred of them!"

"So? What are you saying?" He got that sexy glint in his eyes. There was nothing stopping him.

Two hundred rooms. Even at twice a day. One hundred days of Haley—was that going to be my epitaph?

Anne Boleyn got a thousand days and I only got a tenth of that?

I had to savor every one.

Riggins had promised me two weeks away from the world for our honeymoon. Two weeks at Witham House.

Our days fell into a happy pattern—breakfast in bed, make love, comb the Dead Duke's study for clues, meetings about the estate, rambling over the property and exploring the castle and gardens, dinner, teatime, tea, tea, more tea, always tea, pore over the library, fall into bed and make love again. Repeat the next day.

We worked on our British English, laughing over the differences.

"Death to all articles!" Riggins said to me. "No one here goes to *the* hospital. They go to hospital. They go on holiday. Not on *a* vacation."

I laughed. "Exactly. And yet they take *the* M-5. We just jump on I-5, no *the*. And speaking of differences, I need to go into the village and see the chemist about refilling my one of my prescriptions. Will you come with me? We could have a fun day poking around the shops and town."

He raised an eyebrow. "Can't you send Gibson? We'll be a curiosity."

"You need to get out and meet our neighbors, my darling duke. We can't hole up in this castle forever. In fact, we should have an old-fashioned open house and invite the village people in to meet us."

The village was just behind the castle wall to the rear behind the stables. The land outside the castle walls on the other three sides was all part of the estate for thousands of acres.

He mulled my suggestion over. "Plan something for summer." He paused. "Just be flexible."

What did that mean? Be ready to cancel it if he found a way out?

And so we spent a pleasant afternoon together tooling around the village. We were a curiosity. That was true. But we managed to have the paparazzi snap our picture only about a hundred times or so by actually posing for them, and then enjoyed ourselves in relative peace.

My happiness would have been complete if only Riggins had professed his love. I *thought* he loved me. He acted like a man in love. Or maybe I was only being optimistic and naïve. Sometimes the words seemed to hover on the edge of his lips. Then he'd bite them back.

I'd have been ecstatic if I didn't have to hide my growing love for him. Or if the gap in our differences of opinion about the Dead Duke and the estate weren't widening daily. Where Riggins saw only work and money flying out the window, I saw a life's calling. A mission to preserve history, including family history, and an institution that may have been dying but was so quintessentially English that it seemed worth preserving.

Where he still saw a manipulating old man, I saw a more detailed picture of the Dead Duke emerge. The more I saw, the more I liked him.

The two weeks of our honeymoon flew by. And we'd barely made love in a dozen rooms. No one ever walked in on us. So I assumed Riggins paid the staff off to stay away at appointed times. We also still had thousands of acres to explore, including the hedge maze and poison garden.

Riggins had been trying to convince me to go home with him. I wanted to. Badly. But I was convinced Sid and our interests were better served by me staying. Although she'd rebounded after our weekend at Wareswood, the brief return of her symptoms had scared me. I hadn't finished my work here. I wouldn't be finished until I found what I'd come for.

"I thought coming back to Seattle with me was the plan all along?" Riggins said.

"It was. But we're no closer to finding a cure for Sid or a way to foil the Dead Duke's hold on us than we were when we arrived. If I stay, and don't have you distracting me, I can devote all day to looking through the Dead Duke's paperwork."

"I distract you?" He grinned sexily.

"You know you do." I kissed him. "Come back for our one-month anniversary."

"I don't know if I can wait that long. I'll miss you." His voice broke with emotion.

I believed him. "I'll miss you, too."

It was settled. I'd stay.

The day before Riggins was scheduled to fly out, we slept late.

"You just got adjusted to castle time and now you're going to be off schedule in Seattle, poor baby," I teased.

"Those are the breaks," he said. "I'm used to traveling and being jetlagged."

"So? How are we spending the last day of our honeymoon?" I cuddled up next to him.

"I have something special planned. Dress for walking. I thought we'd take in more of the estate."

Which was how I found myself walking hand in hand with him outside the castle wall, past the maze, down the road, and into the gardens. The grounds had been landscaped by good old Capability Brown. He'd been a busy man in his day. It seemed like he'd designed the grounds of every estate in England.

The weather had cooperated. It was nearly March, but surprisingly clear and warm.

"Where are we going?" I asked Riggins.

"The poison garden."

I stared at him. "Why?"

"Because it's exciting and mysterious."

"And crazy." I shook my head. "Did dukes have food tasters like kings did? Whether they did or didn't, is it just me, or is it crazy to grow poisons right on the grounds? That's like spitting in temptation's eyes, isn't it? Here, heir of mine, poison your duke and take all. Pick your poison—fast-acting or slow. Obvious or subtle."

Riggins laughed as he stopped in front a locked wrought iron gate. The poison garden was clearly labeled, complete with a skull and crossbones sign hanging ominously on the gate like a Halloween decoration.

"Riggins, all this talk of poison just made me think of something. If you die now, with no heirs, the title dies out and goes extinct, but what happens to the castle and real estate? Who inherits it? Me, perhaps?" I batted my eyes at him. But my question was serious.

"I don't think it's in my best interests to answer that." He grinned.

"Well, if it's *not* me, my motivation for becoming a world-class poisoner dwindles to zero." I put on a bright face. "Does that mean it *is* me?"

"I talked to Thorne. If I die without an heir, I can leave the estate to anyone I like."

"And you like me a lot, right?" I batted my eyes again.

He shook his head. "You and the stable cats."

I pouted jokingly. "I really rank." I bumped him with my shoulder. "If you'd been nicer, I might have literally picked your garden-variety poison. Now you'll just have to suffer duchess' choice."

"You're a cruel woman."

"Seriously. Who inherits?"

"I haven't decided what to do with it."

"Oh."

"Hey." He took my chin and tipped my face to his. "Let's not kill the mood."

"No. Definitely not." But I felt unsettled.

"You and Sid will be taken care of, no matter what. Okay?"

I nodded and put on a smile for his benefit. I didn't want to ruin our last hours together. But the mood had been dampened.

He kissed me and pulled a set of keys out of his pocket as he read a posted set of rules for the garden, "No touching; no tasting; no smelling."

"No funning. What are we? Babies? Hands in pockets, children." I laughed. "But seriously—who would use the taste test in a poison garden?

"'Here, darling, just try a bite of this Death Cap mushroom. It's delicious. Don't worry. A mere half will kill you. But if you only *taste* it...'" I shook my head. "You shouldn't even touch those crazy mushrooms."

Riggins unlocked the gate and took my hand, pulling me in, and locking the gate behind us. "The garden's not at its most spectacular in late winter/early spring. But Bird, the gamekeeper, still recommended seeing it.

"We'll come back in summer. I just couldn't resist seeing something so sinister sounding. Since you wouldn't go into the Ghost Tower with me—"

"Well, who would?"

He gave me a suggestive look. "It's got many of the two hundred rooms—"

"No." I shook my head. "I'm not making love in front of a voyeuristic ghost. If you want company in there, you'll have to call your ghost-busting friend Lazer."

Riggins rolled his eyes. "Chicken."

I shrugged. "I'm here in the poison garden, aren't I?" I shuddered with fake fear. "It feels dangerous just being here."

"Wait." I stopped in front of a large bush along the gravel path. "Is that a common rhododendron? We have a ton of those in our garden at home. They're, like, ubiquitous back home. Almost as bad as blackberry bushes. Rhodies are about as deadly as kittens."

"Eat enough of one and it could kill you." He laughed.

"Eat enough of anything and it could kill you. Drink enough water and you could die. But you have to be trying to kill yourself in a completely silly way." I took his arm again. "How deep into the garden are we going?"

"Very deep." His voice was full of innuendo.

"Then I'd better take a very deep breath."

"Why?" He looked genuinely puzzled.

"Rule number three—no smelling." I squeezed his arm. "Way to make a girl breathless, Duke."

He grinned and playfully squeezed me. "You can breathe, just don't smell."

"Stop it!" I laughed and fended him off. "I'm not taking any chances in this dangerous garden. You're going to kill me. You're going to kill us both."

He caught me and kissed me again. "Come on. There's a spot in the garden I want to show you."

The garden was beautifully laid out and arranged. Even in this drab time of year it had spots of color and was peaceful and pretty. We poked along the paths, reading the little signs with plant names. There was foxglove, also known as digitalis, which was used in heart medicine and could be lethal. Opium poppies, which weren't in bloom, obviously, and were illegal in the States. Black cohosh. And all manner of different plants. Including clover, which popped up uninvited. I imagined the gardeners were constantly fighting it.

Riggins seemed eager as he pulled me along the path.

"Is that stinging nettle?" I pointed to a plant along the path. I'd had an unfortunate incident with one at the house. It was growing in one of our planters and I reached in with bare hands to pull it out before I realized what it was. It was aptly named, for sure. "We have that at home, too. Maybe I should have brought gardening gloves. Where are we going?" I laughed as we broke nearly into a run. "What's the rush?"

"I want to show you something."

We came to a spot in the garden full of spring blooms, flowering trees, and flowering early spring bushes bursting with yellows, whites, pinks, and reds.

"Oh." I stopped short, breathless from being with him. "It's like a fairy garden. It's beautiful." I bit my lip to keep from laughing. "But highly deadly, I assume." I raised an eyebrow.

"Naturally. Extremely dangerous if you get off the path." He took me by the shoulders and turned me around. "Look that way. What do you see?"

"The castle!"

It sat proud and tall on the hill above us, looking like something out of a fairytale.

Riggins pulled me close. "When I was seventeen I saw this porno flick about the lord of a castle who had sex with a beautiful maid in the garden."

"Riggins!" I said, pretending to be scandalized as he looked at me lustily. "I'm no maid."

"That you're not." He grinned and ignored me, his breath hot on my hair as he whispered, "Once I became duke and saw this place, I couldn't get the fantasy out of my head. You and me making love in my garden beneath the nose of my castle." He lifted my hair off my neck and nuzzled into me, sucking my neck roughly as if he wanted to brand me.

"You want to act out a porno—"

"I want to have sex with you in the great outdoors." He slid his hands beneath my jacket and T-shirt until they were hot and possessive against my skin. He held me as if he'd never let me go.

I shivered, but it wasn't from cold. And pressed my hands against his chest, feeling his heart beat through his layers of clothes and coat. In that moment, it was mine and beat for me, if only temporarily. And I was damn well going to enjoy it.

I lifted my face to his. He kissed me urgently while I pressed tight against him, feeling his dick hard in his jeans, letting him slide a knee between my legs and rub against me until my panties were wet. And I was aching with desire, too.

"What if someone sees?" My voice went hoarse with desire. But it was less a protest than begging him to act.

"What if they do?" His breath was coming fast. He unzipped my jeans and slid his fingers into my panties and then into me. "You're already ready for me, duchess."

I was. I ached for him as I slid his zipper down and reached into his jeans for him. He was hard. Long. Pulsing.

He unzipped my coat and sucked my nipples through my T-shirt until I groaned with pleasure. "Stop teasing me."

"I thought you'd never ask." He picked me up and laid me on my back in the damp grass. I scrambled to get his dick out of his jeans as he pulled my jeans down over my hips.

Mine, I thought. *For now he's my duke, my man, my husband.*

Overhead the trees were a thick canopy of pink blossoms and blue sky peeking through. The tip of him was wet and slick. As a gentle breeze kicked up, pink petals drifted down on us, and Riggins speared into me, grinding my bare butt and back into the tender grass dotted with dandelions.

With my jeans around my knees, I couldn't lock my legs around him like we liked. Couldn't rock myself against him and squeeze him to me. I had to arch up instead, ceding control to him as he drove into me, holding me tight around the waist to keep me from sliding with each thrust. The breeze carried the gentle scent of the flowers as well as petals.

There we were. Two animals rutting in the orchard of flowering trees. With each powerful thrust, he was more and more mine. Let me be the one to fulfill his teenage fantasy. Let me be the duchess he'd always remember, especially in spring when the trees bloomed.

I held him tight. I could feel the tension build in his arms and back while he pushed me closer and closer to the edge of pleasure. I was waiting for him, trying to match him.

And then I couldn't hold on any longer. I cried out, letting the breeze carry his name and the expression of my pleasure with it.

He grunted and held me tight. I held him as he caught up to me, shuddered, and came.

"Wow." He rested his sweaty forehead against mine. "I I—"

My heart stopped with his words. I felt like I needed a dose of that digitalis. I held my breath, waiting for more. Waiting for the words I was desperate to hear.

"I'll leave tomorrow a happy man." His head was still pressed against mine.

I couldn't see his eyes. He'd caught himself and changed what he was going to say. If only I could have seen his expression.

"Wow is right." I stared up past him at the trees overhead as another shower of petals rained down on us. "And exceptionally dangerous. I think those might be flowering cherries. Everyone knows cherry pits contain cyanide. Cyanide is lethal."

My heart felt brittle, fragile with hope, and desperate for words I might never hear.

"I'm going to miss you." His tone was urgent.

"Then hurry back," I said. "Hurry back to me. There's just one thing..."

"What?"

"How am I going to explain the grass stains on my back?"

He kissed the tip of my nose. "The power of rank— no one questions the duchess."

"But they'll think—"

"What they like."

"One more thing, then." I dusted petals out of his hair. "What kind of orders have you been giving the staff not to walk in on us?"

He grinned. "What are you talking about? I haven't given them any orders at all. That's part of the excitement."

CHAPTER NINE

*R*iggins
I didn't used to believe you could burn for someone. Have an ache for them that was almost physical, like the phantom pain of an amputated limb. As if I was missing a part of myself. Miss the sound of someone's voice so much you sometimes imagined it.

Back in Seattle, that was how I felt about Haley. Hell, who was I kidding? That was how I felt when I pulled away from the castle on my way to the airport. I almost turned back. But that would have been weak. I had obligations in the real world.

But if this wasn't love, it was certainly misery.

I'd almost screwed up in the garden and handed her my heart on a gold platter. Almost told her I loved her.

Damn. I was losing control. What did loving her mean? That I should stay? That we should make a little heir and get on with our life together?

I wasn't ready for that much commitment. I wasn't a forever kind of guy. But Haley was the committed type. Eventually, I would only break her heart.

The best plan seemed to be to just get over it. Get over myself. Get over this stupid notion of falling in love.

I would get over this. I *would*. Nothing good would come from it. People left you. Abandoned you. Disappointed you. I didn't need that shit. Haley didn't need it from me.

I wanted my old life back. I knew where that one was going. I was in control. I didn't need a broken heart. But none of that stopped me from calling or Skypeing her every day. From thinking about her constantly. From suffering endless ribbing.

"The new duchess ditched you already?" were the first words out of Lazer's mouth. And Harry's. And just about every guy I knew. Those or cruder.

I had it bad. I just had to work her out of my system and I'd be myself again. I dove into my work. Worked out for hours each day. And pored over the financials for the castle and estate. Buried in there somewhere had to be the key to getting rid of it before Haley became too attached to it. I didn't like to admit why that mattered, even to myself.

Haley

The Dead Duke was a complicated, mysterious enigma of a man. I decided that in order to find any clues he might have left for me, I had to think like him. I began in the library by reading some of his favorite books, including the family history. One book, a fictionalized account of the first Duke of Witham, back when he was still only an earl, enthralled and amused me. Although it was leather bound and embossed with gold lettering, with pages edged in real twenty-two-karat gold, it was well read and dog-eared. The leather soft with rereading. Certain passages bookmarked.

The first time Gibson showed me the library he'd said *Lady Witham's Great Game* was a favorite of the Dead Duke. There were multiple copies in the collection, the well-worn one being the Dead Duke's personal copy that he had picked up in an antique bookshop when he was a young man. This was how it began:

England
March 1833
There comes a time in the life of every young, newly married countess when she must conceive an heir despite the obstacles fate places in her way—husbands as homely as hoary toads, old men who've joined themselves to youth, but who, to put it delicately, aren't in their full blush of potency. Or possibly even despotic, spoiled men of tolerable age who have no cares for their wife's pleasures.

Scarcely four months into her marriage, Eliza, the seventh Countess of Witham, realized her time was now. If it wasn't too late already.

Henry Feldhem, the odious, perverse, middle-aged, money-grubbing, sweating, blackmailing heir presumptive to her new husband's title, sat on the sofa across from her, hat next to him. He glanced around the drawing room of her husband's countryseat as if it, and everything in Witham House, already belonged to him. Including her.

For just an instant, she wished she were not a countess, but a powerfully built man like Witham who could give the insolent newcomer a good right hook. Instead, she fixed Mr. Feldhem with a cold, cutting gaze.

"What do you mean—my husband is missing?" Despite the shock, she managed to sound calm and almost amused.

All manner of horrible visions—highwaymen, carriage accidents, and lame horses—should have flashed through her mind at Mr. Feldhem's insistence that Witham was not where he told her he was going to be. Namely, London. But sadly, they did not.

What crossed through instead? The exotic landscape of India and Witham on a ship bound for it, leaving her behind. Abandoned. Deserting the nobleman's life he'd never wanted. Faking his death. Returning to whatever adventures he was so fond of in the land where he'd been born and raised.

The passage was so eerily similar to my own situation. Some things never changed. *Produce an heir, girl! Get on it now!* Haha. Really? My duke didn't want one. Although his predecessor had been desperate for one. And still was, from beyond the grave.

Had this book been the inspiration for the Dead Duke's diabolical plans? I laughed at this line: *spoiled men of tolerable age who have no cares for their wife's pleasures.* At least my duke *did* have a care for my pleasures. Boy did he. And he was of more than tolerable age, in his prime.

I couldn't help falling in love with the book and re-reading it. I commandeered the Dead Duke's copy as my own and kept it on my nightstand to read before bed, laughing aloud at the dog-eared pages, cheering for Eliza in her quest to have a baby boy and tame her earl.

What would it be like to have Riggins' baby? To make his heir? Wouldn't that solve all our problems? It was a traitorous thought. Disloyal to my husband in some ways. In others...

Two days after Riggins left, I was poking around the Dead Duke's study—with Riggins' permission and his key—when I found a secret compartment in the Dead Duke's desk.

My hands shook so badly, I could barely open it. Maybe this was where he'd hidden the secret identity of Sid's cure.

I was disappointed. At first, anyway. In it was a stack of letters, love letters, as it turned out, bound with a leather cord. Surprisingly, they were letters the Dead Duke had written *to* Helen. They were post-marked, but returned, unopened. The lovebirds must have had a fight. Interesting. This couple, so romantic and dedicated to each other, had fought so hard that she'd left and refused to read his letters. Which, back in the day, was like ignoring a text, only worse. She probably didn't take his calls, either.

I stared at the letters, debating with myself. Was it right to open them after all these years? Then again, if he hadn't wanted anyone to read them, the wily old duke was deliberate enough in everything he did to destroy them. No, he wanted me, Riggins, *someone*, to find them.

Debate over. I grabbed an antique letter opener and slit carefully through the envelopes, fingers trembling with excitement. As I pulled the beautiful writing paper out, it shook in my hands. I was struck by the Dead Duke's handwriting, how particularly elegant and beautiful it was. He must have had a tyrant of a penmanship teacher.

I read the first letter.

My Darling,

I never should have let you go. A day without you is a day wasted. A day spent wandering in the desert, a lost and thirsty man without his compass. Without his heart.

Today is another day, unremarkable, just like any other. Darker than it should have been, because I could have been loving you. If I hadn't been a coward. If I had confessed my feelings...

Come back to me, darling.

I love you. Desperately. You're breath to me. I can't live without you.

Rans

Those letters were like popcorn, maybe better, totally addictive. I spent the entire afternoon reading, and rereading, them all. Somehow, over the course of a year, Helen had broken the Dead Duke's heart. Like tap-danced on it with her high-heeled shoes. Letter after letter returned unopened.

And Rans, that conniving, cunning old hermit, had been a true romantic down to his soul, which he poured out on the page. He couldn't fake something like that in letters like these.

So our manipulator, Rans the Dead Duke, who seemed almost like two different people in my mind, had neglected to tell Helen how he felt about her? And lost her for over a year? I made a note to ask Gibson if he knew anything about it.

The Dead Duke's letters to Helen made me wonder if I was making a similar mistake. Should I tell Riggins I loved him and take my chances?

I had been gradually ingratiating myself with the staff. Talking to them. Getting to know them. Asking them zillions of questions about the estate, the Dead Duke, the village. I was hoping to build their trust and find out what they knew in general. Hoping something would slip. I'd talked to pretty much everyone but Bird, the gamekeeper. He was always out on the estate and seemed to think, from what Gibson told me, that the game was purely Riggins' domain. I didn't see how he would be much help to me, anyway.

That evening before Gibson retired for the night, I asked him about the Dead Duke and Helen. "I found some letters in the late duke's desk." I was trying to be more respectful of the Dead Duke around the staff, who seemed to have loved him. I explained my find. "To your knowledge, did the late duke and Helen break up for a time before they married? Do you know anything about it?"

Gibson nodded. "I heard the stories, of course, ma'am. The young duke had to marry for money to save the estate. Helen had money. The story I heard was that she fell madly in love with him. But came to believe he wanted her only for her money.

"I can't blame her for thinking so. It was a common enough practice in those days for a financially strapped British noble to look for an American heiress to marry. She refused his initial offer of marriage and returned to Seattle, I believe, for over a year. Until he finally went to Seattle himself and convinced her he loved her. She finally accepted his marriage proposal. It's a romantic tale, ma'am."

"Yes." I frowned. "So they married in 1934." I'd been piecing the family history together. "And had their first baby in 1939. Helen died a few days after of a hemorrhage."

"I believe so," Gibson said.

"Odd that there were no babies in five years." I was still puzzling it out. Helen had been only twenty when they married. And the Dead Duke twenty-three. They should have been fertile enough.

"There were many miscarriages, I believe."

"Ah." I nodded. "That makes sense. Poor thing."

"The Rh factor is what the doctors eventually suspected. The late duke had O-positive blood. The late duchess, the rare B-negative. They were doomed. The young heir was likely the only child they would have had that lived."

I bit my lip and frowned harder. "But usually, without treatment, only the first child is unaffected. After the first baby, the mother's body builds up antibodies that attack the developing baby. Which explains the miscarriages."

"They got lucky having the one who lived." Gibson nodded. "Though he lived less than a year. The official cause of death was a childhood fever of some sort. But he was a sickly baby. Very likely he had heart problems from birth and wouldn't have lived to adulthood."

"That's tragic." It really was. I had more and more sympathy for the Dead Duke. How much loss could one man take?

"Yes. Broke the late duke's heart to lose his son. The baby was the last bit of Helen he had. And losing his only heir was a blow, too. He insisted on a blood test before marrying either of the second two duchesses, even though by then there were treatments for the Rh difference. There was no Rh factor problem between them."

I sighed. "Sadly, it didn't make a difference. No more babies for him." I had a thought. "Did the other two duchesses miscarry?"

"No, ma'am. Both barren, as I understand it."

Riggins was supposed to fly back for our one-month anniversary. Instead, Kayla went into labor. Riggins had to stay in Seattle to run Flash while Justin was out.

I could have flown over, but I was feeling under the weather. Tired. And he was swamped, anyway. I stayed at Witham House, frustrated in my search for Sid's cure. Where was that elusive twin? And who would know anything about him or her? I met the locals. Listened to their stories of the castle, the Dead Duke, his family. Nothing. Nothing. Nothing! Rose, to my chagrin, became a regular guest at the castle. Suddenly, she was my best friend. That was what she reported on social media, anyway. She was also dating a wealthy older man. A sugar daddy? Maybe. But as long as she was out of my hair, I was happy for her. Though I still didn't trust her.

The more I got to know the Dead Duke, the more convinced I was he knew *something* that could help Sid. It may very well have been the twin that Mr. Thorne thought existed and I was desperate to find. But the Dead Duke had hidden whatever knowledge he had well, leaving only a cryptic, vague treasure map for me to puzzle out. At times, I hated him for keeping the cure from me.

He wanted that heir. And was determined to withhold the prize until he got it. I wanted my sister to have a long, healthy life.

At others, I loved the old man. Or, more correctly, the young, romantic man. And admired the way he'd saved the castle and lovingly restored it.

Two days after our one-month anniversary, Gibson announced Riggins' cousin, Maggie Feldhem, had arrived to see me. I hadn't invited her. It was bold of her to come. I met with her as briefly as possible. It was an unpleasant affair.

I told Riggins about her visit that evening.

"What the hell was Maggie thinking?" His frustration with her came through loud and clear. "Did she want money?"

"Oh, so you do know your cousin!" I laughed, although it wasn't funny. "Oh, yeah. She not only wanted money, she made some not-so-veiled threats she promised to act on if she didn't get some. She threatened to contest the will.

"She claims she can have your dad's death certificate revoked because his body was never recovered. And the investigation reopened."

"How? Let me get this straight—she thinks she can have him re-declared alive? That's bullshit."

"With the estate in the balance, she thinks she can. She hinted you had motive to get rid of your dad once you realized what you stood to inherit if he was out of the picture."

Riggins snorted. "Right. I was in Seattle. I didn't even know where he was or that he was dead. Or missing."

"She can open a can of worms. If he was alive, he'd be the duke and you'd lose it all—"

"She's blackmailing me?" He laughed. "Did you tell her she should have done her research? That she'd be giving me what I want? That would have shut her up."

"Riggins! This is serious. She says she can make you look bad. And petition for her share of the money that your dad would have given her. Because she was his favorite niece. And by him being declared dead, she was cheated out of her rightful inheritance."

"Eh. She's all bluster. She only goes for the easy money. Everything she described is too much work and too iffy. She doesn't have the money for a big court battle, anyway. Or the connections or patience. As we know, the will's airtight. I'm sure the Dead Duke thought of every contingency. She doesn't have a prayer."

"It points out one thing—you need a will." I hesitated. "Or an heir."

There was a heavy pause in the conversation. I shouldn't have brought it up.

"It would break my heart if someone like Maggie got the estate," I said. "She'd ruin it in the space of minutes. Spend every penny and bankrupt the place. Throw outrageous parties that trash it. You can't let that happen, Riggins. *Please.* Be responsible about this—"

He sighed. "I won't let it happen. I promise."

"Don't die before you do. Don't die *ever.*" I let my emotion into my voice. Damn him. Why couldn't he see that the easiest solution was for us to have a child? I was wanting one more and more. It was like living here had cast a maternal spell on me.

The Feldhem dynasty needed a new generation to keep things going. Someone with Riggins' drive, intelligence, and charm. And I *wanted* to have his baby. Couldn't he see how much I loved him and wanted to provide that for him? I couldn't even imagine him having a baby with anybody else.

"I'll try not to. But I'll die eventually." His voice was soft. "I miss you. Desperately. Get well and come home to Seattle."

"How desperately?" I tried to sound light. "Do you feel like a man wandering in the desert, lost and thirsty, without his heart?"

"Worse." His voice was so damn sexy. "I'm parched. Have you been reading the Dead Duke's letters again?"

"Hey, you could learn something from them, duke." My voice had a harder, more desperate edge than I'd intended.

"Are you saying I'm not romantic enough?"

I might have been reading too much into it, but he sounded almost hurt beneath his trademark amusement.

"I'm saying I miss you, too. In the worst way. As soon as I find some hope of Sid's cure..."

I swallowed hard. I missed Sid, too. Maybe I could bring her out for spring break and we could look for clues together. "It feels like Rans is keeping it just out of reach until I give him what he wants."

"Rans? Are you on a first-name basis with the Dead Duke now?" Riggins didn't sound happy. He sounded almost worried.

"It's easier and kinder than Dead Duke, isn't it? It *was* his name." Why was I so defensive? Tears stung my eyes, both of frustration and sentimentality. I was awfully emotional these days and working on a tightly wound string.

"Huh."

"He wasn't *all* bad, Riggins."

"No. Probably not."

"Let's not argue," I said.

"No. Let's not."

It would have been the perfect time to say I love you. But he didn't. And neither did I.

CHAPTER TEN

Haley

A week later, Alice gave me a worried look when I came into the kitchen for something to settle my stomach. "You don't look madly keen for your breakfast this morning, ma'am."

The sight of my full English breakfast and those stewed tomatoes on the plate she held out to me was almost enough to make me toss my cookies. These days I ate only the toast.

"No. Sorry. I think I have a bug. My stomach's been touchy lately."

Alice pursed her lips. "You should see the doctor."

"Hmmmm. Maybe."

"The chemist, then. See if he has anything for your stomach."

More like a pregnancy test. I was late. Not very. It could just be that I was in for a rough period. My breasts were sore. They'd never done that before. Anyway, what were the odds I'd be pregnant? Birth-control pills were ninety-nine percent reliable and I'd taken them faithfully. Hadn't missed one. No, that was highly unlikely. What if I had an ovarian cyst or something? Sometimes I could be a bit of a hypochondriac.

"Maybe I'd better make you some peppermint tea today? It settles the stomach." She looked to me for affirmation.

"Yes." I nodded. "That sounds wonderful. And how about a dry piece of toast? I can make that myself—"

"No. Don't trouble yourself. That's my job." She gave me a knowing look.

"I don't know what's wrong with me. I've only come down here a few times to bake since the duke left. That's not like me at all. I love baking. I wanted to learn the secret to that sticky toffee pudding."

Alice smiled to herself. "There's plenty of time for that when you're feeling up to it."

No, it couldn't be what she was thinking.

But as I left the kitchen after nibbling my toast, I wondered. I really needed a pregnancy test. There was no point in going to the village for one. Everyone would find out and the rumors would fly. I could pull rank and ask one of the maids who came in regularly to buy one for me. But, again, who could I trust? I finally decided to order one online. Just for peace of mind. I didn't need it immediately, anyway. A few days were nothing to wait.

It turned out I was wrong. Two days was an eternity to wait. When the test finally arrived late in the afternoon a few days later, I grabbed it from Gibson and ran to my rooms, locking the door behind me.

I actually trembled as I read the directions. This was silliness. I wasn't pregnant. I couldn't be. No one was that fertile. The odds were completely against me. I wasn't even *trying*.

Mornings were better for test accuracy. But afternoons were fine if you'd missed your period. And I had. I had extra tests anyway if this one was inconclusive. I was too impatient to wait.

Riggins would be so furious if I was pregnant. So disappointed. I took a deep breath and headed to the bathroom. I sat on the toilet and stuck the stick in the stream. It lit up positive immediately. I wasn't only pregnant. I was definitely, positively pregnant. Bursting with pregnancy hormones.

I sat on the toilet and put my head between my knees, alternating between joy and terror. If only the Dead Duke were here. *He* would be thrilled. But Riggins?

Oh crap. I'd have to tell him. Eventually. But what would he think—that I'd trapped him? That we were going to have not a shotgun wedding but a shotgun marriage?

I took a deep breath. I had to think. How had this happened? How had our birth control failed so miserably?

And what if the baby was a girl? If we'd been trying to get pregnant, we would have taken steps to up our odds of having a boy. Even guarantee it.

My phone rang. I jumped like a guilty kid and pulled it from my pocket, dreading a call from Riggins for the first time ever.

It was Gibson. "Ma'am, Lady Rose is in the drawing room waiting to see you."

Yes, Rose. I didn't mind her as much as I thought I would. She was always gushing about us being family. So much so that I had a hard time putting her off. I'd temporarily forgotten she was coming today. Something about a favor she needed. Just what *I* needed.

"Yes. Thank you, Gibson. I'll be right down."

I quickly dried my eyes with the back of my hand and sucked it up.

Rose was waiting for me, casually looking at the paintings around the room. "Haley." She hugged me. "Just browsing and thinking. I've always loved this place. How are you?" Her expression turned to concern. "You look pale. Have you seen a ghost?"

I should have applied more blush. I smiled. "Not quite. But spending time with the late duke's things is almost as bad. It's like he's still here."

Gibson was just finishing setting up tea. "Can I get you anything before I go, ma'am?"

"We're fine, Gibson. Thank you." I poured Rose and me each a cup and handed her hers, a small sandwich plate, and a pair of tongs.

"It looks delicious. As always. You're so lucky to have good staff here. The late duke was a perfectionist and a lovable tyrant, I heard. But he knew how to get good, loyal staff and keep them." She looked beautiful, like always.

I felt a mess. My tangled emotions must have shown on my face. Which made me feel even more insecure as I served myself a small cucumber sandwich. I begged to differ with her. Everything on the tray made my stomach turn. Especially the egg salad and smoked salmon sandwiches. Just a whiff of them made me gag. Something about the smell of eggs...

I added a plain scone to my plate and sat on the sofa next to Rose, setting my goodies on the coffee table in front of us. "You wanted to see me about something? A favor?"

I didn't know how long I could last through tea. I wanted to make sure we got to whatever had brought her over. She'd caught me at a bad time, both physically and emotionally.

She looked pained and almost embarrassed. She sighed prettily. "Yes, a big favor, I'm afraid. I'm not at all chuffed at asking." She bit her lip.

Why was she acting all coy? Riggins wasn't here, and nor were any of his billionaire friends. There were no white knights ready to dance attendance on her.

"I may as well come out with it. I need money. Lots of it. A couple million pounds. And I can't go to my boyfriend for it right now. I've already tapped him out. I don't want to scare him off by asking him for more. Or give him any ideas that all I want is his money." Her laugh was brittle. "He's already leery." She took a deep breath. "I'm desperate. My father is on the brink of foreclosure."

She gave me a look that I was certain was supposed to elicit my sympathy and bring on my guilt. Intimating that if I hadn't won *her* prize, she wouldn't be in this situation.

"In the long run, he needs a couple million pounds. In the near term, if he doesn't come up with at least several hundred thousand pounds immediately, he'll lose our ancestral home. It's been in the family hundreds of years. The humiliation of being the earl who lost the estate. And after his father and grandfather weathered the world wars and the heavy tax increases...well, I'm sure you understand."

Her statement was pointed and to the point. Almost barbed, but desperate at the same time. How could I, an American from the middle class, understand anything like that? And yet after just a little more than a month here, I did. To a degree, at least.

"You want money?" Of course she wanted money. She'd just said so. I was having trouble concentrating. My stomach turned over. The scent of her perfume, usually subtle and classy, was cloying and nauseating. The room felt too close.

I took a deep breath. "I know it sounds ridiculous, but I don't have *any* money. It's all Riggins'."

"No inheritance?" She must have been as desperate as she claimed. She was pressing hard.

I shook my head. "Some is held in trust. If certain conditions are met, I'll get it eventually. The late duke didn't hand out his money readily. If you'd like to ask Riggins..."

I got a whiff of the egg salad sandwiches and salmon. Bile rose in my throat. I gagged. My stomach lurched. There was no time to run across the castle to the loo, as they called it here. I grabbed the nearest handy receptacle, a tall vase, and retched into it, mortified.

When I was finished, I felt better. Rose was clutching her throat. Her eyes were narrow. She handed me a napkin.

I took it and wiped my mouth as she studied me closely.

"You're pregnant," she said at last.

I shook my head.

"Don't lie to me. I know a pregnant woman when I see one."

I looked away and put the napkin over the mouth of the vase. "Please don't mention this...incident...to anyone. It's embarrassing. I apologize. I'm sure you've lost your appetite. We can move across the room."

She was still staring at me. "Does Riggins know?"

I changed the subject. "I'm sorry for your financial situation. I know what it is to need money. I can talk to him for you if you like." I tried to smile, even though I felt horrible and shaken.

She received a text just then. She pulled her phone from her purse, frowned, and texted something back. "I don't have time to wait for him." She gave me an accusing look. "My stupid, optimistic, naïve papa! He left this to the last minute. My stupid siblings are no help. It's up to me. I only have hours."

"I have about ten thousand pounds I can give you." I could take it out of the household funds.

"Thank you. But it's not nearly enough. I'll just have to take matters into my own hands."

Riggins

I'd been fooling myself, trying to convince myself I wasn't in love with my wife. At night I burned for her. By day I yearned to hear her voice and see her smile. I was a desperate man. Being separated from her made me see that what I felt wasn't a temporary crush. I missed Haley too damn much to stay in denial. Something had to give—my pride.

I was in love with her. In *love* with my duchess. A woman the Dead Duke had foisted on me. A wife I hadn't wanted.

I never pictured myself getting married in the first place. Never wanted a wife. Or children. Or any of that crap.

Children? The thought made me shudder. I would be such a shitty dad. My douche of an old man had done a number on me. A number I wasn't about to replicate on a future generation. *What a legacy.* Kids had never been in my plans. Still weren't. The Feldhem line deserved to die out. The estate could be a legacy for the British people, a museum from a bygone era. I'd will it to them. In the meantime, I was going to have a hell of a fun time being the last Duke of Witham with my duchess.

So what did Haley and I do now? Where did we go from here?

All I knew was that I had to get back to Witham House before she fell more in love with the place.

Me, in love? *Crazy.* Fate must have been having a good laugh at my expense.

It certainly seemed that absence really *did* make the heart grow fonder. Or maybe it only drew a big fat circle around what was true love and who was being an idiot for denying it.

Suddenly, I was desperate to tell Haley. To say the words *I love you.* A hell of thing to be feeling almost two months after the wedding.

I realized with a start that I'd never really been in love before. Not like this. Sure, first love. In college. But not filled with want of this depth. With missing her. With needing to be with her and feeling incomplete without her.

I had no idea what this meant for our future. Or even if she loved me back. Did this mean I wanted our marriage to be real?

It was too soon to decide that. I just knew I had to tell her how I felt and worry about the rest later.

Flash would have to do without me for a few days. I needed to show Haley how romantic I could be. I decided to surprise her with a visit. I chartered a private plane and headed for Witham House with my heart pounding and a smile on my face.

Haley
I was mortified. Horrified. Humiliated. Exhausted.

Rose hurried off. Probably to hit someone else up for money. I emptied and rinsed the vase before Gibson or one of the cleaning staff found it. What did I do now? I was going to have to tell Riggins, and soon. In some romantic way? Apologetically?

The pregnancy test was nearly one hundred percent accurate when it gave a positive result. But maybe having it verified by a doctor would add validity to my claim. Should I see a doctor? How did the British medical system work? Was there an obstetrician in the village?

I wanted my mom. I always missed her. But now I really missed her. I'd gotten used to playing mom to Sid. Now I needed a mom myself. She'd know what to do. But I was on my own.

I wanted to go home. I had to go home to Seattle, where I could see my family ob/gyn. Where I knew how things worked and who I could trust. I needed to tell Riggins. In person. As soon as possible.

All my fears and insecurities flooded in. How would he take it? Would he throw me out of the castle? How would I hide my morning sickness from him until after I'd seen the doctor?

I wanted to talk to Sid and tell her so badly. But I felt, deep down, that the daddy-to-be deserved to be the very first person to know. No matter how afraid I was of the consequences, Riggins had the right to be the first to hear the news. I hadn't even verified it to Rose.

I had told Rose the truth on the other score, though. I didn't have any real money of my own. But I had enough pin money to book a first-class flight home. I made a plan. I'd fly home. See my doctor. And surprise Riggins afterward. It was already evening, but Seattle was eight hours behind us. My doctor's office back home would be open. I called and made an appointment for Friday morning. If I flew in on Thursday and spent the night at a hotel... Yes, I just might be able to pull it off. I grabbed my laptop and booked my flight online. Exhausted, I snuggled into bed with my latest find from the Dead Duke's study, an old Bible that had belonged to his mother. The Bible had been incongruously placed on a shelf of books on farming, business, and estate management. I hadn't noticed it at first. The books hadn't interested me as much as the files. Truthfully, they hadn't interested me at all.

But Bibles sometimes contained records of birthdates and death dates, that kind of thing. And this one was pretty when you finally noticed it. The fact that it was his mother's might have had some significance, so I had carted it back to my room. Maybe his mother had some wisdom to give me.

As I leafed through it, it fell open to a page with a yellowed letter tucked inside, still in its original envelope. The return address was from my great-great-aunt, Helen's sister and my great-grandmother, to Rans. It was postmarked the year I was born.

His name and address were written in spidery, old-lady handwriting on the envelope, as if it had taken a lot of effort to compose. From the condition of the envelope, it appeared the letter was as well read and loved as his copy of *Lady Witham's Great Game*.

After Riggins went back to Seattle, I'd had Gibson bring a small TV into the room so I could watch it late at night. I had it on to one of the late night entertainment shows, playing in the background.

I was filled with excitement as I carefully pulled the letter out of its envelope. "What were you doing hiding in the Bible, darling?" I whispered to it as I unfolded it and began reading.

I paled. I couldn't believe what it said. "No, this can't be true. It changes *everything*." I felt sick again.

You know how no matter how distracted you are or absorbed in something, if you hear your name it brings you right out? The entertainment news host on the TV said my name.

"Haley, Duchess of Witham, is pregnant, a close friend of the duchess revealed exclusively to *Entertainment Britain*. It's not official yet, but expect an announcement from the duke and duchess soon.

"The duchess is already experiencing morning sickness and reportedly retched into a priceless antique vase during a friend's very recent visit..."

Rose. I was going to kill her. That was why she hurried away this afternoon. No doubt she sold the story. Were the details of my life really worth several hundred thousand pounds? What did I do now?

Riggins
The car was waiting for me at the airport. I could hardly wait to see Haley again. I had a dozen roses, and

the sexiest, most exclusive lingerie I could find. Too
clichéd? What else could I do? What said *I love you* in
just the right romantic way? Should I have brought
jewelry and chocolate, too?

We pulled up to the front entrance of the castle. My
heart pounded. I wasn't a coward, but the thought of
rejection left a bitter taste of fear in my mouth. Was I
really going to lay my heart on the line and make myself vulnerable to her? Because love sure as hell made
me do stupid things. Would I bare my soul, too?

I imagined myself throwing open the castle door and
announcing, *Honey! I'm home.* But who the hell would
hear me?

She was probably in a room with a moose. I'd have
to text her to track her down. I kept imagining the
surprised, happy look on her face when she realized I
was here. In England. That I loved her.

Was it too much to hope she loved me, too? Had I
misread the signals?

There was a TV in the car. I hadn't been paying any
attention to it. Until I heard Haley's name.

Haley

I ran to the bathroom and threw up until my stomach was empty. This time, I didn't feel better at all. I
was just as shaken and sick as before. I brushed my
teeth and curled up in bed. What was I going to do?
Was there any chance Riggins had seen this? Who else
had picked it up? What if some reporter asked him for
a comment?

I was just grabbing my cell phone to call him when the door to the bedroom flung open.

I jumped, hand to heart.

Riggins stood in the door, his eyes flashing. "Is it true? Are you pregnant?"

Gina Robinson is the award-winning author of the romantic comedy Switched at Marriage serial, contemporary new adult romances *Rushed, Crushed, Hushed, Reckless Longing, Reckless Secrets,* and *Reckless Together* and the Agent Ex series of humorous romantic suspense novels. She's currently working on the next Jet City Billionaire romance.

Connect with Gina Online:
My Website: http://www.ginarobinson.com/
Twitter: @ginamrobinson
Facebook: www.facebook.com/GinaRobinsonAuthor

Made in United States
Orlando, FL
22 August 2022

21405302R10095